H. Strange

A Medical directory for the province of Ontario, 1869

H. Strange

A Medical directory for the province of Ontario, 1869

1st Edition | ISBN: 978-3-75250-273-2

Place of Publication: Frankfurt am Main, Germany

Year of Publication: 2020

Salzwasser Verlag GmbH, Germany.

Reprint of the original, first published in 1869.

A

MEDICAL DIRECTORY

FOR

THE PROVINCE OF ONTARIO,

1869.

PREPARED FOR THE INFORMATION OF THE MEDICAL PROFESSION BY

H. STRANGE, M. D.

PRINTED BY C. E. STEWART, PUBLISHER, HAMILTON.

1869.

PREFACE.

Since the repeal of what was known as DR. PARKER'S Act, I ve been frequently asked for copies of the new Act, and in consequen f my inability to supply this demand I am continually being appealed to information connected with the working of the Act,—especially with regard to the manner of holding the Elections, and the mode of procedure to be adopted in prosecuting illegitim Practitioners.

This demand has been so great, that I have been quite unable to give satisfactory information by letter. In fact the pressing nature of my official and private duties have not left me time to attend to these matters. I have, therefore, been induced to publish the Act, with short commentaries upon those parts which have been the most frequent subjects of enquiry.

In the hope of making this pamphlet more useful, I have added the By-law passed by the Medical Council at its late session, relating to the lections of representatives in the Council of the Territorial Divisions.

The constitution of these constituencies is in many cases difficult to comprehend, on account of the alterations made by the British North American Act in the boundaries of many of the Counties. In order to meet this difficulty I have prepared an accurate description of the boundaries, so that there need be no difficulty in knowing exactly what is comprised in each Division.

There will also be a list of all registered Practitioners entitled to vote at the Medical Elections corrected up to the moment of going to press, with their respective addresses, and the Division in which they reside.

Besides what has been enumerated above, there will be several other matters included, which will render this pamphlet a complete Directory of information which it is important for every Medical Practitioner in Ontario to have in his possession.

H. STRANGE, M. D.

Hamilton, May 20th, 1869.

ONTARIO MEDICAL ACT.

An Act to Amend and Consolidate the Acts relating to the Profession of Medicine and Surgery.

[*Assented to 23rd January*, 1869.]

WHEREAS, it is expedient to amend and consolidate the Acts relating to the medical profession, and to make more effectual provision for regulating the qualifications of practitioners of medicine, surgery and midwifery, and to incorporate the medical profession of Ontario: Therefore, Her Majesty, by and with the advice and consent of the Legislative Assembly of the Province of Ontario, enacts as follows:— Preamble.

I. The Act of the Parliament of the late Province of Canada, twenty-nine Victoria, chapter thirty-four; the Act chapter forty-one of the Consolidated Statutes of Upper Canada; the Act passed in the twenty-fourth year of Her Majesty's reign, chapter one hundred and ten; and all Acts amending any of the said Acts, are hereby repealed; and the provisions of this Act shall stand in the place of the provisions of the said Acts; but all proceedings heretofore taken, and all matters and things done under the said Acts, shall be valid and effectual notwithstanding such repeal, and may be carried on and completed under this Act as effectually as they could have been under the said Acts. Acts 29 Vic., chap. 34; chap. 41, Con. Stat. U. C.; 24 Vic., chap. 110, and Acts amending same repealed.

II. The Council and Boards established, and the Members thereof elected under the provisions of the Acts repealed, shall be continued, and shall act until after the first election as hereinafter provided, but subject in all other respects to the provisions of this Act; and all by-laws, rules and regulations heretofore made by the said Council and Boards, shall remain in force until repealed or modified under the provisions of this Act. Council and Boards previously elected, and by-laws, etc., to be continued, etc.

III. The officers appointed under the provisions of the Act first above mentioned, shall retain their respective offices, and perform their respective duties under the provisions of this Act; and all books and registers heretofore kept by them in conformity with the Act hereby repealed, shall be continued in use for their respective purposes under this Act. Officers formerly appointed to retain office, etc.

IV. The repeal of the said Act twenty-nine Victoria, chapter thirty-four, of the late Province of Canada, shall not have the effect of reviving the Acts repealed by it, nor of modifying or restricting in any way whatsoever, the saving effect of the thirty-sixth section thereof. Repealed Acts not revived.

V. This Act may be cited as "The Ontario Medical Act." Title of Act.

College of Physicians and Surgeons of Ontario.

VI. The Medical Profession of Ontario is hereby incorporated under the name and style of "The College of Physicians and Surgeons of Ontario," and shall have a corporate seal; and every person registered according to the provisions of the Act twenty-nine Victoria, chapter thirty-four, and the Acts amending the same, shall be, and is hereby made a member of the said College of Physicians and Surgeons of Ontario; and every person who may be registered hereafter, under the provisions of this Act, shall be a member of the said College.

Council of Ontario, etc.

VII. There shall be a "Council of the College of Physicians and Surgeons of Ontario," to be appointed in the manner hereinafter provided for in this Act, and referred to in this Act as the "Council."

How composed.

VIII. The Council shall be composed as follows: Of one member to be chosen from each of the Colleges and bodies hereinafter designated, to wit: University of Toronto, Queen's University and College of Kingston, University of Victoria College, University of Trinity College, Royal College of Physicians and Surgeons of Kingston, Toronto School of Medicine, and of every other College or body in the Province now by law authorized, or which may be hereafter authorized to establish a Medical Faculty in connection therewith, and to grant degrees in Medicine and Surgery, or other certificates of qualification to practise the same: Provided always, that no teacher, professor or lecturer of any of the before mentioned colleges or bodies shall hold a seat in the Council except as a representative of the college or body to which he belongs.

Proviso.

Additional members thereof.

2. There shall also belong to the said Council five Members to be elected by the duly licensed practitioners in Homœopathy, who have been registered under this Act; and five members to be elected by the duly licensed practitioners in the Eclectic system of Medicine, who have been registered under this Act.

Certain members to be residents of territorial divisions.

3. The twelve Members who shall be elected in the manner hereinafter provided from amongst and by the registered Members of the Profession, other than those mentioned in the next preceding sub-section, shall be residents of the several Territorial Divisions for which they are elected.

Members to be registered practitioners.

IX. All Members of the Council, representing the Colleges or bodies in the eighth section mentioned, shall be practitioners duly registered under this Act, or the before mentioned Act.

One from each territorial division, etc.

X. Of the twelve Members to be elected from amongst the registered practitioners of Medicine in the Province of Ontario, one shall be so elected for each of the Territorial Divisions mentioned in Schedule C to this Act annexed, by the registered practitioners resident in such division; and the manner of holding such election shall, with respect to the time thereof, and the taking of the votes therefor, be determined by a by-law to be passed at the next meeting of the Council; and in default of such by-law being made, then the Lieutenant Governor shall prescribe the time and manner of such election.

Provision as to period of election, and as to resignation, death, etc., of Members of Council.

XI. The Members of the Council shall be elected or appointed, as the case may be, for a period of three years; but any Member may resign his appointment at any time by letter addressed to the President or Registrar of the Council; and upon the death or resignation of any Member of the Council, it shall be the duty of the Registrar forthwith to notify the College or body, wherein such vacancy may occur, of such death or resignation, and such College or body shall have the power to nominate another duly qualified person to fill such vacancy, or if the vacancy be caused by the death or resignation of any member elected from the Territorial Divisions, the Registrar shall forthwith cause a new election to be held in such Territorial Division by a notice to be published in the Ontario *Gazette*, and in, at least, three newspapers, published in the said Division, for, at least, one month, fixing the time and place for holding such election; and such election shall be conducted in accordance with the By-laws and regulations of the Council; but it shall be lawful for the Council during such vacancy to exercise the powers hereinafter mentioned.

Provision in case of death, etc., of representative of Homœopathic or Eclectic systems.

2. In the event of the death or resignation of any member of the Council representing the practitioners in Homœopathy or the Eclectic system of Medicine, it shall be lawful for the remaining representatives of Homœopathy or the Eclectic system of Medicine in the Council to fill such vacancy by selecting a person from among the duly registered practitioners in Homœopathy or the Eclectic system of Medicine, as the case may be.

First election.

XII. The first election under this Act for Members to represent the Territorial Divisions in the Council, shall take place on the second Tuesday in June, one thousand eight hundred and sixty-nine, at such places in the several divisions as shall be fixed by by-law of the Council; and it shall be the duty of the Registrar to cause a notice of the time and place for holding the said elections to be published in the Ontario *Gazette*, and in at least three newspapers in each of the said divisions for at least one month before the said second Tuesday in June.

First election of representatives of Homœopathic and Eclectic systems.

2. The first election under this Act for Members to represent the duly licensed and registered practitioners in Homœopathy and the Eclectic system of Medicine in the Council, shall take place on the second Tuesday in June, one thousand eight hundred and sixty-nine, in such manner and at such place or places as shall be fixed by by-law of the Council; and it shall be the duty of the Registrar to cause a notice of the time and place for holding the said elections, to be published in the Ontario *Gazette* for at least one month before the said second Tuesday in June; and in default of such by-law being made, then the Lieutenant-Governor shall prescribe the terms and manner of such election.

First meeting of newly elected Council.

XIII. The said newly elected members of the Council, as well as all members of the Council to be hereafter elected, shall, together with the members to be appointed by the several Colleges and bodies as mentioned in section eight of this Act, hold their first meeting on the second Wednesday in July next after the said election in the City of Toronto, at such place as may be fixed by by-law of the retiring Council.

Subsequent elections.

XIV. Every subsequent election shall be held on the second Wednesday in June, in every third year after the said first election, in the same manner as is provided for holding the first election as aforesaid.

Who entitled to vote.

XV. The persons entitled to vote at any election under this Act, shall be the Practitioners duly registered under this Act.

Time, place, etc., of holding meetings.

XVI. The Council shall hold its first meeting under this Act, in Toronto, and at such time and place as the President of the Council, or, in case of his absence or death, the Registrar for the time being shall appoint therefor, and shall make such rules and regulations as to the times and places of subsequent meetings of the Council, and the mode of summoning the same as to them shall seem expedient, which rules and regulations shall remain in force till altered at any subsequent meeting; and in the absence of any rule or regulation as to the summoning of future meetings of the Council, it shall be lawful for the President thereof, or, in the event of his absence or death, for the Registrar to summon the same, at such time and place as to him shall seem fit, by circular letter to be mailed to each member: Provided always, that at least two weeks' notice of such meeting be given; and in the event of the absence of the President from any meeting, the Vice-President, or in his absence, some other member to be chosen from among the members present, shall act as President; and all the acts of the Council shall be decided by the majority of the members present, the whole number not being less than nine; and at all meetings, the President, for the time being, shall have a casting vote only.

Future meetings.

Proviso.

Quorum.

Expenses of members.

XVII. There shall be paid to the members of the Council such fees for attendance, and such reasonable travelling expenses, as shall from time to time be fixed by by-law passed by the said Council.

Officers of College, etc.

XVIII. The Council shall annually appoint a President, Vice-President, and a Registrar and Treasurer, who shall hold office during the pleasure of the Council, and such other officers as may, from time to time, be necessary for the working of this Act; and the said Council shall have power to fix, by by-law or from time to time, the salary or fees to be paid to such Registrar and Treasurer, and to the Board of Examiners hereafter appointed.

Funds to be paid to Treasurer.

XIX. All moneys forming part of the Council funds, shall be paid to the Treasurer, and shall be applied to carry this Act into execution.

Medical Registration.

Register book to be kept, containing names of all persons complying with Act.

XX. The Council shall cause to be kept by an officer appointed by them, and to be called the Registrar, a book or register in which shall be entered, from time to time, the names of all persons who have complied with the enactments hereinafter contained, and with the rules and regulations made or to be made by the Council respecting the qualifications to be required from practitioners of Medicine, Surgery and Midwifery in this Province; and those persons only whose names have been, or shall hereafter be inscribed on the book or register above mentioned, shall be deemed to be qualified and licensed to practise Medicine, Surgery or Midwifery in the Province of Ontario, except as hereinafter provided; and such book or register shall at all times be open, and subject to inspection by any duly registered practitioner in Ontario, or by any other person.

XXI. It shall be the duty of the Registrar to keep his register correct, in accordance with the provisions of this Act, and the rules, orders and regulations of the Council, and to erase the names of all registered persons who shall have died; and he shall, from time to time, make the necessary alterations in the addresses or qualifications of the persons registered under this Act; and to enable him duly to fulfil the duties imposed on him, it shall be lawful for him to write a letter to any registered person, addressed according to the address of such person on the register, to enquire whether he has ceased to practise or has changed his residence; and if no answer shall be returned to such letter within the period of six months from the sending of such letter, it shall be lawful for the Registrar to erase the name of such person from the register: Provided always, that the same shall be restored by direction of the Council, upon cause duly shown to that effect; and the said Registrar shall perform such other duties as shall be imposed upon him by the Council.

Duty of Registrar.

Proviso.

XXII. Every person now possessed, or who may, within the period of six months from the passing of this Act, become possessed, of any one or more of the qualifications described in the schedule A to this Act, shall, on the payment of a fee, not exceeding ten dollars, be entitled to be registered, on producing to the Registrar the document conferring or evidencing the qualification, or each of the qualifications in respect whereof he seeks to be so registered, or upon transmitting by post to the Registrar, information of his name and address, and evidence of the qualification or qualifications in respect whereof he seeks to be registered, and of the time or times at which the same was or were respectively obtained; and any person entitled to be registered before the first day of July, one thousand eight hundred and sixty-five, may, on complying with the requirements in this section mentioned, obtain such registration on payment of a fee of five dollars: Provided he register within one year after the passing of this Act: Provided also, no one registered under the Act first above mentioned shall be liable to pay any fee for being registered under this Act.

Provision for registry of all persons properly qualified.

Proviso.

Proviso.

XXIII. Every person desirous of being registered under the twentieth section of this Act, and who shall not have become possessed of any one of the qualifications in the said schedule A mentioned, before the expiration of the period of six months after the passing of this Act, shall, before being entitled to registration, present himself for examination as to his knowledge and skill for the efficient practise of his profession, before the Board of Examiners in the next section mentioned, and upon passing the examination required, and proving to the satisfaction of the Board of Examiners that he has complied with the rules and regulations made by the Council, and on the payment of such fees as the Council may determine, such person shall be entitled to be registered, and, in virtue of such registration, to practise Medicine, Surgery and Midwifery in the Province of Ontario: Provided always, that when and so soon as it shall appear that there has been established a Central Examining Board, similar to that constituted by this Act, or an Institution

Person not qualified until six months after passing of Act to be examined before committee, etc.

Proviso.

duly recognized by the Legislature of any of the Provinces forming the Dominion of Canada, other than Ontario, as the sole examining body, for the purpose of granting certificates of qualification, and wherein the curriculum shall be equal to that established in Ontario; and the holder of such cerificate shall, upon due proof, be entitled to registration by the Council of Ontario, if the same privilege be accorded by such Examining Board or Institution to those holding certificates in Ontario.

Persons practising before Jany. 1st, 1850.

2. Any person who was actually practising Medicine, Surgery or Midwifery, or any of them, in Ontario, prior to the first day of January, one thousand eight hundred and fifty, and who shall have attended one course of lectures at any recognized Medical School, shall, upon such proof as the Council may require, be entitled to registration under this Act.

Provision for admission of Homœopathic and Eclectic practitioners.

3. Any person who was actually practising Medicine, Surgery or Midwifery, according to the principles of Homœopathy or the Eclectic system of medicine, before the first day of January, one thousand eight hundred and fifty, and for the last six years in Ontario, may, in the discretion of the representatives of the Homœopathic or Eclectic systems of medicine, be admitted to register under this Act.

Council to appoint committee to examine candidates.

XXIV. At the first regular meeting of the Council, after the passing of this Act, and at the annual meeting in each year thereafter, there shall be elected by the members of the said Council, a Board of Examiners, whose duty it shall be to examine all candidates for registration, in accordance with the by-laws, rules and regulations of the Council; such examinations to be held at Toronto and Kingston, and at the same time as examinations for matriculation of students-

Time and place for examinations.

Board of examiners, how composed.

XXV. The Board of Examiners appointed under the preceding section, shall be composed as follows: One Member from each of the three teaching bodies now existing in Ontario, and one from every other School of Medicine which may be hereafter organized in connection with any University or College which is empowered by law to grant medical or surgical diplomas: and nine Members to be chosen from among those Members of the College of Physicians and Surgeons of Ontario, who are unconnected with any of the above teaching bodies: Provided always, that every candidate who shall, at the time of his examination, signify his wish to be registered as a Homœopathic or Eclectic practitioner, shall not be required to pass an examination in either Materia Medica or Therapeutics, or in the Theory or Practice of Physic, or in Surgery or Midwifery, except the operative practical parts thereof, before any examiners other than those approved of by the represcntives in the Council of the body to which he shall signify his wish to belong.

Proviso.

Council to make orders, as to registers, fees, examining committees, etc.

XXVI. The Council shall, from time to time, as occasion may require, make orders, regulations or by-laws for regulating the registers to be kept under this Act, and the fees to be paid for registration; and shall, from time to time, make rules and regulations for the guidance of the Board of Examiners, and may prescribe the subjects and mode of the examinations, the times and places of holding the same, and generally, may make all such rules and regulations in respect of such examinations, not contrary to the provisions of this Act, as they may deem expedient and necessary; such examinations to be both oral and written; and shall also make by-laws and regulations appointing returning officers, and directing the manner in which elections shall be conducted, and the expenses of the same paid for.

XXVII. Any person entitled to be registered under this Act, but who shall neglect or omit to be so registered, shall not be entitled to any of the rights or privileges conferred by the provisions of this Act so long as such neglect or omission continues.

Persons not registered, not entitled to privileges, etc.

XXVIII. If the Registrar make or cause to be made any wilful falsification in any matter relating to the register, he shall incur a penalty of fifty dollars, and shall be disqualified from again holding that position.

Wilful falsification by Registrar.

Medical Education.

XXIX. Every person registered under this Act, who may have obtained any higher degree or any qualification, other than the qualification in respect of which he may have been registered, shall be entitled to have such higher degree or additional qualification inserted in the register in substitution for, or in addition to, the qualification previously registered, on the payment of such fee as the Council may appoint.

Provision as to persons obtaining higher qualification than that registered.

XXX. No qualification shall be entered on the register, either on the first registration or by way of addition to a registered name, unless the Registrar be satisfied by proper evidence that the person claiming is entitled to it; and any appeal from the decision of the Registrar may be decided by the Council, and any entry which shall be proved to the satisfaction of the Council to have been fraudulently or incorrectly made, may be erased from the register by an order in writing of the Council: Provided always, that in the event of the Registrar being dissatisfied with the evidence adduced by the person claiming to be registered, he shall have the power, subject to an appeal to the Council of refusing the said registration until the person claiming to be registered shall have furnished such evidence, duly attested by oath or affirmation before the Judge of the County Court of any County in Ontario.

No qualification to be registered unless Registrar satisfie.

Proviso.

XXXI. Every person who shall be registered under the provisions of this Act, shall be entitled, according to his qualification or qualifications, to practise Medicine, Surgery, and Midwifery, or any of them, as the case may be, in the Province of Ontario, and to demand and recover in any Court of law, with full costs of suit, reasonable charges for professional aid, advice and visits, and the cost of any medicine or other medical or surgical appliances rendered or supplied by him to his patients.

Every one registered may practise, and recover his fees, etc.

XXXII. The Registrar of the Council shall, from time to time, under the direction of the Council, cause to be printed and published, a correct register of the names in alphabetical order according to the surnames, with the respective residences, in the form set forth in Schedule B to this Act or to the like effect, together with the medical titles, diplomas and qualifications conferred by any college or body, with the dates thereof,

Registrar to cause correct register to be published of names, etc., of persons registered with particulars, etc.,

of all persons appearing on the register as existing on the day of publication; and such register shall be called "*The Ontario Medical Register*;" and a copy of such register for the time being, purporting to be so printed and published as aforesaid, shall be *prima facie* evidence in all Courts, and before all Justices of the Peace and others, that the persons therein specified are registered according to the provisions of this Act; and the absence of the name of any person from such copy shall be *prima facie* evidence that such person is not registered according to the provisions of this Act: Provided always, that in the case of any person whose name does not appear in such copy, a certified copy under the hand of the Registrar of the Council, of the entry of the name of such person on the register, shall be evidence that such person is registered under the provisions of this Act.

Proviso.

Council may appoint examiners, etc., for matriculation examinations.

XXXIII. The Council shall have power and authority to appoint an examiner or examiners for the admission of all students to the matriculation or preliminary examination, and to make by-laws and regulations for determining the admission and enrollment of students; and the following shall be the subjects for such matriculation or preliminary examination: Compulsory,—English Language, including Grammar and Composition; Arithmetic, including Vulgar and Decimal Fractions; Algebra, including Simple Equations; Geometry, first two books of Euclid; Latin translation and Grammar; and one of the following optional subjects: Greek, French, German, Natural Philosophy, including Mechanics, Hydrostatics, and Pneumatics.

Subjects of examination.

Graduates of Colleges in other Provinces not required to pass matriculation examination on producing certificate, etc.

2. It shall not be necessary for students graduating in any College in any of the Provinces forming the Dominion of Canada, other than Ontario, to pass the matriculation or preliminary examination in Ontario, prior to being examined by the Board of Examiners, as provided in the twenty-third section of this Act, if the person presenting himself for examination shall produce a certificate showing that he has passed a matriculation or preliminary examination at the College where he may have graduated, equal to that prescribed by the Council in Ontario.

What other persons exempted.

3. Any graduate, or any student, having matriculated in Arts in any University in Her Majesty's Dominions, shall not be required to pass the preliminary examination.

Council to fix curriculum of studies.

XXXIV. The Council shall have power and authority to fix and determine from time to time a curriculum of studies to be pursued by students, and such curriculum of studies shall be observed and taught by all colleges or bodies referred to in section eight of this Act: Provided always, that such curriculum of studies shall first receive the approval of the Lieutenant Governor in Council, and be published once in the Ontario *Gazette*; and that no change in the curriculum at any time existing shall come into effect until six months after the first publication in the said Ontario *Gazette*.

Proviso.

Penal and General Clauses.

Registered practitioner convicted of felony.

XXXV. Any registered medical practitioner, who shall have been convicted of any felony in any Court, shall thereby forfeit his right to registration, and, by the direction of the Council, his name shall be erased from the register ; or in case a person known to have been convicted of felony, shall present himself for registration, the Registrar shall have power to refuse such registration.

Fees not to be recovered unless registration proved.

XXXVI. No person shall be entitled to recover any charge in any Court of law for any medical or surgical advice, or for attendance, or for the performance of any operation, or for any medicine which he shall have prescribed or supplied, unless he shall prove upon the trial that he is registered under this Act.

Interpretation of certain words.

XXXVII. The words "legally qualified medical practitioner," or "duly qualified medical practitioner," or any other words importing legal recognition of any person as a medical practitioner or member of the medical profession, when used in any Act or law shall, in so far as such Act or law applies to this Province, be construed to mean a person registered under this Act.

Registration necessary for appointment to hospitals, etc. ;

XXXVIII. No person shall be appointed as medical officer, physician or surgeon in any branch of the public service of the Province of Ontario, or in any hospital or other charitable institution, not supported wholly by voluntary contributions, unless he be registered under the provisions of this Act.

and for validity of certificates.

XXXIX. No certificate required by any Act now in force, or that may hereafter be passed, from any physician or surgeon or medical practitioner, shall be valid, unless the person signing the same be registered under this Act.

Penalty for persons wrongfully procuring registration.

XL. If any person shall wilfully procure, or attempt to procure, himself to be registered under this Act by making or producing, or causing to be made or produced, any false or fraudulent representation or declaration, either verbally or in writing, every such person so offending and every person knowingly aiding and assisting him therein, shall incur a penalty of fifty dollars.

Punishment of persons falsely pretending to be physicians.

XLI. Any person who shall wilfully and falsely pretend to be a physician, doctor of medicine, licentiate in medicine or surgery master of surgery, bachelor of medicine, surgeon or general practitioner, or shall practice medicine, surgery or midwifery, for hire, gain or hope of reward, or shall falsely take or use any name, title, addition or description, implying, or calculated to lead people to infer that he is registered under this Act, or that he is recognised by law as a physician surgeon or accoucheur, or a licentiate in medicine, surgery, or midwifery, or a practitioner in medicine, shall, upon a summary conviction before any Justice of the Peace, for any such offence, pay a sum not exceeding one hundred dollars, nor less than twenty-five dollars.

Members of council to notify death.

XLII. It shall be the duty of the member of the council representing each territorial division to notify the Registrar of the Council of the death of any registered medical practitioner occurring within his division, so soon as he shall become aware of the same ; and upon the receipt of such notification, the Registrar shall erase the name of the person so deceased from the register.

How penalties recovered.

XLIII. All penalties imposed by this Act shall be recoverable, with full costs of suit, by the Council in the name of the College of Physicians and Surgeons of Ontario.

SCHEDULE A.

1. License to practise Physic, Surgery and Midwifery, or either, within Upper Canada, granted under the Acts of Upper Canada, fifty-nine George the Third, chapter thirteen, and eight George the Fourth, chapter three, respectively.

2. License or diploma granted under the second Victoria, chapter thirty-eight, or under the Consolidated Statutes for Upper Canada chapter forty or any Act amending the same.

3. License or authorization to practise Physic, Surgery and Midwifery, or either, within Lower Canada, whether granted under the ordinance twenty-eight George the Third, chapter eight, or under the Act ten and eleven Victoria, chapter twenty-six, and the Acts amending the same, or under chapter seventy-one of the Consolidated Statutes for Lower Canada, or any Act amending the same.

4. Certificate of qualification to practise Medicine, Surgery and Midwifery, or either, hereafter to be granted by any of the colleges or bodies named or referred to in section [four] eight of this Act.

5. Medical or surgical degree or diploma of any University or College in Her Majesty's dominions, or of such other Universities or Colleges as the Council may determine.

6. Certificates of registration under the Imperial Act, twenty-one and twenty-two Victoria, chapter ninety, known as "The Medical Act," or any Act amending the same.

7. Commission or warrant as Physician or Surgeon in Her Majesty's Naval or Military Service.

8. Certificates of qualification to practise under any of the Acts relating to Homœopathy or the Eclectic system of medicine.

SCHEDULE B.

Name.	Residence.	Qualifications and additions.
A. B.	Toronto, Co. of York.	M.A., M.D., Toronto University.
C. B.	Kingston, Co. of Frontenac	M.A., M.D., Queen's University
E. F.	Etobicoke, Co. of York.	Licentiate, Medical Board.
G. H.	Toronto	do Toronto School of Medicine.

SCHEDULE C.

1. Western and St. Clair Electoral Divisions, as established previous to the Confederation of the British American Provinces, for election of Members of the Legislative Council of the late Province of Canada.

2. Malahide and Tecumseh Electoral Divisions, as established previous to the Confederation of the British American Provinces, for election of Members of the Legislative Council of the late Province of Canada.

3. Saugeen and Brock Electoral Divisions, as established previous to the Confederation of the British American Provinces, for election of Members of the Legislative Council of the late Province of Canada.

4. Gore and Thames Electoral Divisions, as established previous to the Confederation of the British American Provinces for election of Members of the Legislative Council of the late Province of Canada.

5. Erie and Niagara Electoral Divisions, as established previous to the Confederation of the British American Provinces, for election of Members of the Legislative Council of the late Province of Canada.

6. Burlington and Home Electoral Divisions, as established previous to the Confederation of the British American Provinces, for election of Members of the Legislative Council of the late Province of Canada.

7. Midland and York Electoral Divisions, as established previous to the Confederation of the British American Provinces, for election of Members of the Legislative Council of the late Province of Canada.

8. King's and Queen's Electoral Divisions, as established previous to the Confederation of the British American Provinces, for election of Members of the Legislative Council of the late Province of Canada.

9. Newcastle and Trent Electoral Divisions, as established previous to the Confederation of the British American Provinces, for election of Members of the Legislative Council of the late Province of Canada.

10 Quinté and Cataraqui Electoral Divisions, as established previous to the Confederation of the British American Provinces, for election of Members of the Legislative Council of the late Province of Canada.

11. Bathurst and Rideau Electoral Divisions, as established previous to the Confederation of the British American Provinces, for election of Members of the Legislative Council of the late Province of Canada.

12. St. Lawrence and Eastern Electoral Divisions, as established previous to the Confederation of the British American Provinces, for election of Members of the Legislative Council of the late Province of Canada.

A BY-LAW

To regulate the Elections in the twelve Electoral Divisions described in Schedule C of the Medical Act.

Passed April 8th, 1869.

Whereas, power has been granted to the Medical Council, in the Ontario Medical Act, to make By-laws for determining the manner of holding the elections under the said Act, be it therefore enacted as follows :—

I.—This By-law does not apply to the election of Homœopathic or Eclectic Members of the Council.

II.—The elections of Members to represent the Territorial Divisions referred to in section twelve of the Ontario Medical Act, shall be held respectively in the places mentioned in Schedule A to this By-law.

III.—There shall be no nomination for the position of Member of the Council.

IV.—It shall be the duty of the Registrar to transmit to each registered Medical Practitioner a voting paper, printed according to the form given in Schedule B to this By-law. The said voting paper shall be filled up by the Voter in favor of the candidate of his choice, and shall be forwarded to the Returning Officer of the Division in which the Voter resides, in a sealed envelope. Each envelope shall have a printed address, by which the Returning Officer may recognize its character; and such paper shall not be examined, nor such envelope opened until the day appointed for recording these votes.

V.—No votes shall be accepted after two o'clock in the afternoon of the second Tuesday in June, at which time the voting papers shall be carefully examined by the Returning Officers, and a correct record kept of each legal vote given. After all the votes have been recorded, the Returning Officer shall add up the votes given, and declare the Candidate who has received the largest number of votes to be duly elected, to serve as member for the Division.

VI.—In case two or more candidates receive an equal number of votes, the Returning Officer shall give the casting vote, for one of such candidates, and his vote shall decide the election.

VII.—It shall be the duty of the Returning Officer to make a certificate over his hand of the result of the election, and shall transmit the same to the Registrar of the Council, within the three days next following the day of election, together with all the papers connected therewith; and the Registrar shall keep the said papers, as the property of the Council.

VIII.--In the event of the death, or unavoidable absence, or refusal to act, of any Returning Officer appointed by the Council, it shall be lawful for the present Representative of such Division to appoint a Returning Officer in place of the one appointed by the Council.

SCHEDULE A.

No. and Name of Division.		Name of Returning Officer.	R[illegible]ence of [illegible]g Officer.
No. 1	Western and St. Clair. ..		Chatham.
No. 2	Malahide and Tecumseth.		London.
No. 3	Saugeen and Brock......		Guelph.
No. 4	Gore and Thames.......		Woodstock
No. 5	Erie and Niagara........		Brantford.
No. 6	Burlington and Home...		Hamilton.
No. 7	Midland and York.......		Toronto.
No. 8	King's and Queen's......		Whitby.
No. 9	Newcastle and Trent.....		Cobourg.
No. 10	Quinté and Cataraqui....		Kingston.
No. 11	Bathurst and Rideau....		Ottawa.
No. 12	St. Lawrence and Eastern.		Brockville.

SCHEDULE B.

The name of the Candidate for whom your vote is cast:

Residence of the Candidate:

Name in full of Voter,......................................

Residence of Voter, ______

County of Voter,.................. Riding,..................

Territorial Division,......................................

I,............________..........of the

..........................of..........................

do solemnly affirm that I am registered under the Medica[l] Act, and that the date of such registration is..................

Signed,......................................

Witnessed by

....

Justice of the Peace.

TERRITORIAL DIVISIONS.

There always was some degree of difficulty in finding out the exact boundaries of many of the Electoral Divisions, on account of the Ridings of Counties being separated—one Riding being sometimes in one Division and another Riding in another Division. Great as this difficulty was at the time of the first election, it is infinitely greater now, on account of the changes which have been made in the boundaries of many Counties and Ridings by the British North American Act, 1867.

Many Counties have had portions cut off and allotted to new Counties, while others, which formerly had two Ridings, are now divided into three; such, for instance, as Hastings, Middlesex and Wellington.

The Electoral Divisions, as constituted for the purposes of the Medical Act, are as they were for elections to the Legislative Council in the late Province of Canada; but as every one has not copies of the Consolidated Statutes at hand, it may be of service to have the composition of the Territorial Divisions printed in this form. It is believed that the composition of the Divisions, as here given may be relied upon, for it has been prepared with great care, and has cost an immense amount of labor, in compiling from the Statutes.

Towns and Villages which have been incorporated since the fourth day of May, 1859, are not specifically mentioned here, but are to be taken as forming parts of the Ridings or Counties within which they may be locally situate.

For the legal boundaries of Counties, as they are formed for the purposes of the Ontario Medical Act, see the Act, Chapter 3, *Consolidated Statutes of Upper Canada.*

For the legal boundaries of Ridings, as formed for the purposes of the Ontario Medical Act, see Chapter 2, *Consolidated Statutes of Canada.*

No. 1.—WESTERN AND ST. CLAIR.

WESTERN DIVISION.

Essex, County of.

Kent, do.

Camden, Township of.	Orford, Township of.
Chatham, do.	Raleigh, do.
Dover East, do.	Romney, do.
Dover West, do.	Tilbury East, do.
Howard, do.	Zone, do.
Harwich, do.	

And the Town of Chatham.

ST. CLAIR DIVISION.

Lambton, County of.

Bosanquet, Township of.
Brooke, do.
Dawn, do.
Enniskillen, do.
Euphemia, do.
Moore, do.
Plympton, do.
Sarnia, Township of.
Sombra, do., including Walpole Island, St. Anne's Island, and the other Islands at the mouth of the River St. Clair.
Warwick, Township of.

And the Town of Sarnia.

Middlesex, do. (*West Riding.*)

Mosa, Township of.
Carradoc, do.
Adelaide, do.
West Williams, do.
Delaware, do.
Eckfrid, Township of.
Metcalfe, do.
East Williams, do.
Lobo, do.

No. 2.—MALAHIDE AND TECUMSETH.

MALAHIDE DIVISION.

Elgin, County of, (*East Riding.*)

Bayham, Township of.
Yarmouth, do.
Malahide, Township of.
South Dorchester, do.

And the Village of St. Thomas.

Elgin, County of, (*West Riding.*)

Southwold, Township of.
Aldborough, do.
Dunwich, Township of.

Middlesex, County of, (*East Riding.*)

West Nissouri, Township of.
Westminster, do.
North Dorchester, do.
London, do.

London, City of.

TECUMSETH DIVISION.

Huron, County of.

Ashfield, Township of.
Biddulph, do.
Colborne, do.
Grey, do.
Goderich, do.
Hay, do.
Howick, do.
Hullett, do.
McGillivray, do.
McKillop, Township of.
Morris, do.
Stephen, do.
Stanley, do.
Turnberry, do.
Tuckersmith, do.
Usborne, do.
Wawanosh, do.

And the Town of Goderich,
and the Village of Clinton.

Perth, County of

No. 3.—SAUGEEN AND BROCK.

SAUGEEN DVISION.

Bruce, County of.

Arran, Township of.		Elderslie, Township of.	
Amable,	do.	Greenock,	do.
Albemarle,	do.	Huron,	do.
Brant,	do.	Kinloss,	do.
Bruce,	do.	Kincardine,	do.
Culross,	do.	Lindsay,	do.
Carrick,	do.	Saugeen,	do.
Eastnor,	do.	St. Edmund,	do. together with

all that portion of the Peninsular Tract of land known as the Indian Reserve, and not included in the County of Grey, and the Islands in Lake Huron and the Georgian Bay contiguous thereto.

And the Villages of Walkerton and Southampton.

Grey, County of.

Artemesia, Township of.		Melancthon, Township of.	
Bentinck,	do.	Normanby,	do.
Collingwood,	do.	Osprey,	do.
Derby,	do.	Proton,	do.
Euphrasia,	do.	Sydenham,	do.
Egremont,	do.	Saint Vincent,	do.
Glenelg,	do.	Sullivan,	do.
Holland,	do.	Sarawak,	do. together with
Keppel	do.		

[exclusive of the Townships of Keppel and Sarawak] that portion of the Peninsular Tract of land known as the Indian Reserve, and situated between lines drawn northward from the north-east angle of Arran, and the north-west angle of Derby, until they respectively strike Colpoy's Bay, on the east side of the Indian Village, and waters of the Georgian Bay, and the Islands contiguous thereto.

And the Town of Owen Sound.

Simcoe, do. (*North Riding.*)

Nottawasaga, Township of.		Sunnidale, Township of.	
Vespra,	do.	Flos,	do.
Ora,	do.	Medonte,	do.
Orillia,	do.	Tiny,	do.
Tay,	do.	Matchedash,	do.
Muskoka,	do.	Balaklava,	do.
Robinson,	do.		

And the Town of Barrie.

BROCK DIVISION.

Wellington, County of, (*North Riding.*)

Nichol, Township of. Garafraxa, Township of.
Pilkington, do. Peel, do.
Arthur, do. Maryborough, do.
Amaranth, do. Luther, do.
Minto, do.

Wellington, County of, (*South Riding.*)

Guelph, Township of. Puslinch, Township of.
Erin, do. Eramosa, do.

And the Town of Guelph.

Waterloo, County of, (*North Riding.*)

North Waterloo, Township of. Woolwich, Township of.
Wellesley, do.

And the Town of Berlin.

No. 4.—GORE AND THAMES.

GORE DIVISION.

Waterloo, County of, (*South Riding.*)

SouthWaterloo, Township of. North Dumfries, Township of.
Wilmot, do.

And the Town of Galt, and the Village of Preston.

Oxford, County of, (*North Riding.*)

East Nissouri, Township of. East Zorra, Township of.
West Zorra, do. Blandford, do.
Blenheim, do.

And the Town of Woodstock.

THAMES DIVISION.

Oxford, County of, (*South Riding.*)

North Oxford, Township of. West Oxford, Township of.
East Oxford, do. North Norwich, do.
South Norwich, do. Dereham, do.

Norfolk, County of

No. 5.—ERIE AND NIAGARA.

ERIE DIVISION.

Brant, County of, (*East Riding.*)

South Dumfries, Township of. Onondaga, Township of
East Brantford, do.

And the Village of Paris.

ERIE DIVISION.—(*Con.*)

Brant, County of, (*West Riding*)

Burford, Township of.	Oakland, Township of.
Tuscarora, do.	West Brantford, do.

And the Town of Brantford.

Haldimand, County of.

North Cayuga, Township of.	Oneida, Township of.
South Cayuga, do.	Rainham, do.
Canborough, do.	Seneca, do.
Dunn, do.	Sherbrooke, do.
Moulton, do.	Walpole do.

And the Village of Caledonia.

NIAGARA DIVISION.

Lincoln, County of.

Clinton, Township of.	Gainsborough, Township of.
Caistor. do.	Louth, do.
Grimsby, do.	Niagara, do.
Grantham, do.	

And the Towns of Niagara,
Queenston, and
St. Catharines.

Welland, County of.

Bertie, Township of	Stamford, Township of.
Crowland, do.	Thorold, do.
Humberstone, do.	Willoughby, do.
Pelham, do.	Wainfleet, do.

And the Town of Clifton.

And the Villages of

Chippewa,	Thorold, and
Fort Erie,	Welland.
Merrittsville,	

No. 6.—BURLINGTON AND HOME.

BURLINGTON DIVISION.

Wentworth, County of, (*North Riding.*)
Wentworth, do. (*South Riding.*)
Hamilton, City of.

HOME DIVISION.

Halton, County of.
Peel, do.

Albion, Township of.	Toronto, Township of.
Caledon, do.	Toronto Gore, do.
Chinguacousy, do.	

And the Villages of Brampton and
Streetsville.

No. 7.—MIDLAND AND YORK.

MIDLAND DIVISION.

York, County of, (*North Riding.*)

King, Township of.
Whitchurch, Township of.
Georgina, do
East Gwillimbury, do.
North Gwillimbury, do.

Simcoe, County of, (*South Riding.*)

West Gwillimbury, Township of.
Tecumseth, Township of.
Innisfil, do
Essa, do.
Adjala, do.
Tossorontio, do.
Mulmur, do.
Mono, do,

YORK DIVISION.

Toronto, City of

And the Township of York.*

No. 8.—KINGS AND QUEENS.

KINGS DIVISION.

York, County of, (*East Riding.*)

Markham, Township of.
Scarborough, Township of.

York, County of, (*West Riding.*)

Etobicoke, Township of.
Vaughan, Township of.

Ontario, County of, (*South Riding.*)

Whitby, Township of.
East Whitby, Township of.
Pickering, do.

And the Town of Whitby.

And the Village of Oshawa.

QUEEN'S DIVISION.

Ontario, County of, (*North Riding.*)

Reach, Township of.
Uxbridge, Township of.
Brock, do.
Scott, do.
Thorah, do.
Mara, do.
Rama, do.
Scugog, do.

Victoria, County of.

Durham, do. (*West Riding.*)

Clarke, Township of.
Darlington, Township of.
Cartwright, do.

---

* The Township of York was divided into Eastern and Western portions (by Yonge Street,) which were respectively attached to the East and West Ridings of York for electoral purposes, under the Act relating to representation in the Legislative Assembly. But in the Act relating to the Legislative Council, the Township of York is specifically excluded from King's Divsion (which embraced both Ridings of York), and it is specifically included in York Division.

The Incorporated Village of Yorkville, though geographically situate in the township of York, is not specifically excluded from King's Division, as the Township of York is. It is, therefore, very difficult to decide whether it should be considered a part of York Division, or a part of King's Division.

In the opinion of the compiler, the intention of the law was to include Yorkville in the Township of York, he has therefore interpreted it as being included, though not specifically mentioned.

No. 9.—NEWCASTLE AND TRENT.

NEWCASTLE DIVISION.

Durham, County of, (*East Riding.*)

Cavan, Township of.	Manvers, Township of.
Hope, do.	

And the Town of Port Hope.

Northumberland, County of, (*East Riding.*)

Cramahe, Township of.	Brighton, Township of.
Murray, do.	Seymour, do.
Percy, do.	

Northumberland, County of, (*West Riding.*)

Hamilton, Township of.	Haldimand, Township of.
Alnwick, do.	South Monaghan do.

And the Town of Cobourg.

TRENT DIVISION.

Peterborough, County of.

Hastings, do. (*North Riding.*)

Lake, Township of.	Tudor, Township of.
Grimsthorpe, do.	Marmora, do.
Madoc, do.	Elzevir, do.
Rawdon, do.	Huntingdon, do.
Hungerford, do.	McClure, do.
Herschel, do.	Faraday, do.
Wallaston, do.	Wicklow, do.
Monteagle, do.	Dungannon, do.
Limerick, do.	Bangor, do.
Carlow, do.	Mayo, do.
Cashel, do.	

Lennox, County of.

Adolphustown, Township of.
North Fredericksburgh, do.
South Fredericksburgh, do.
Richmond, do.

And the Village of Napanee.

No. 10.—QUINTE AND CATARAQUE.

QUINTE DIVISION.

Hastings, County of, (*South Riding.*)

Sydney, Township of.	Thurlow, Township of.
Tyendinaga, do.	

And the Town of Belleville,
And the Village of Trenton.

Prince Edward, County of.

Cataraque Division.

Addington, County of

Anglesea, Township of.	Ernesttown, Township of.
Amherst Island, do.	Kalader, do.
Camden, do.	Sheffield, do.

Frontenac, County of

Barrie, Township of.	Loughborough, Township of.
Bedford, do.	Olden, do.
Clarendon, do.	Oso do.
Howe Island. do.	Portland, do.
Hinchinbrooke, do.	Palmerston, do.
Kennebec, do.	Pittsburgh, do.
Kingston, do.	Storrington do.

Wolfe Island, (including Simcoe Island, Garden Island, Horse Shoe Island, and Mud Island.)

And the City of Kingston

No. 11.—BATHURST AND RIDEAU.

Bathurst Division.

Leeds, County of, (*South Riding.*)

Rear of Yonge and Escott, Township of.
Front do. do.
Front of Escott, do.
Front of Leeds and Lansdowne, do.
Rear do. do. do.

South Crosby, Township of.	North Crosby, Township of.
Bastard, Township of	Burgess, Township of.

Bathurst Division.—(*Con.*)

Lanark, County of, [*North Riding.*]

Sherbrooke North, Township of.	Dalhousie, Township of.
Lanark, do.	Ramsay, do.
Lavant, do.	Darling, do.
Pakenham, do.	

Lanark, County of, [*South Riding.*]

Montague, Township of.	Elmsley North,Township of.
Burgess North, do.	Sherbrooke South, do.
Beckwith, do.	Drummond, do
Bathurst, do.	

And the Town of Perth.

Rideau Division.

Renfrew, County of.
Carleton, do.
Ottawa, City of.

No. 12.—ST. LAWRENCE AND EASTERN.

St. Lawrence Division.

Brockville, Town of.
Elizabethtown, Township of.
Grenville, (*South Riding.*)
Edwardsburgh, Township of. Augusta, Township of.
And the Town of Prescott.
Leeds and Grenville, Counties of, (*North Riding.*)
Kitley, Township of. Elmsley, Township of.
Wolford do. Oxford, do.
South Gower do.
Dundas, County of.

Eastern Division.

Stormont, County of.
Prescott, do.
Russell, do.
Glengarry do.
Cornwall, Town of
and the Township of Cornwall.

LIST OF VOTERS.

A List of persons registered under the provisions of the Ontario Medical Act, who are legally entitled to vote for a Representative in the Council of a Territorial Division. 1869

No. of Div.	NAME.	TITLE.	ADDRESS.	COUNTY.
5	Aberdein, Robert	LRCS.; Ed.	*Chippawa*	Welland.
12	Addison, Robt. Wm	M. D	*Farmersville*	Leeds.
10	Agnew, John	M. D	*Portsmouth*	Frontenac.
2	Agnew, John Washington.	LRCS.; Ed.	*London*	Middlesex.
7	Agnew, John Noble	M. D	*Toronto*	York.
1	Agnew, Niven	M. D	*Delaware*	Middlesex.
5	Aiken, Edward	M. D	*Hullsville*	Haldimand.
6	Aikins, Moses Henry	M. B	*Burnhamthorpe*	Peel.
7	Aikins, Wm. Thomas	M. D	*Toronto*	York.
6	Aikman, Robert	M. D	*Wellington Square*	Halton.
5	Alexander, James Adam	M. D	*St. Catharines*	Lincoln
7	Allan, James	C M	*Toronto*	York.
11	Allan, Joseph	LFPS; Glas	*Osgoode*	Carleton.
6	Allison, Samuel	M. D	*Caledon East*	Peel.
8	Allison, Wm.	LFPS; Glas	*Bowmanville*	Durham.
1	Allworth, Edward	M. D	*Kingsville*	Essex.
5	Alway, Enoch	M. D	*Smithville*	Lincoln.
5	Alway, James William	M. D	*Smithville*	Lincoln.
11	Anderson, Wm. J.	M. D	*Smith's Falls*	Lanark.
1	Andrews, Alfred Augustus.	L. M. B	*Windsor*	Essex.
2	Appleton, Robert	MRCS; Eng	*Clinton*	Huron.
3	Ardagh, Arthur	MRCS; Eng	*Barrie*	Simcoe.
3	Ardagh, John	MRCS; Eng	*Barrie*	Simcoe.
3	Ardagh, John	MRCS; Eng	*Orillia*	Simcoe.
11	Armstrong, Albert	M. D	*Arnprior*	Renfrew.
10	Armstrong, Alfred	M. D	*Wolfe Island*	Frontenac.
7	Armstrong, John	M. D	*Rosemont*	Simcoe.
8	Armstrong, Thomas	L. M. B	*Brougham*	Ontario.
7	Armstrong, Thomas Mahon	L. M. B	*Rosemont*	Simcoe.
1	Askin, Charles Jas. Stewart	L. M. B	*Chatham*	Kent.
6	Atkinson, Edward Lewis	M. D	*Hamilton*	Wentworth.
4	Ault, John M.	L.M.B	*Tillsonburg*	Oxford.
10	Aylsworth, Archibald K.	M. D	*Newbury*	Addington.
9	Aylsworth, Isaac Brock	L. M. B	*Cobourg*	Northumberland.
12	Aylsworth, Robert Bowen.	M. D	*Lansdowne*	Leeds.
4	Bain, James	M. D	*Ayr*	Waterloo.
3	Barnhart, Charles Edward	M. B	*Owen Soumd*	Grey.
3	Barnhart, John	L. M. B	*Owen Sound*	Grey.
3	Barr, John	M. D	*Horning's Mills*	Grey.
7	Barrett, Michael	L. M. B	*Toronto*	York.
7	Barrick, Eli James	M. D	*Toronto*	York.
8	Bascom, Joseph	M. B	*Uxbridge*	Ontario.
5	Baxter, Benjamin	M D	*Cayuga*	Haldimand.
5	Baxter, Jacob	M. D	*Cayuga*	Haldimand.
10	Beamish, William	M. D	*Waterloo K'n*	Frontenac.
4	Beard, Geo. L.	L. M. B	*Norwich*	Oxford.
3	Beaton, Alex. H.	M. D	*Stayner*	Simcoe.
11	Beatty, Daniel	M. D	*Richmond*	Carleton.
9	Beatty, John	M. D	*Cobourg*	Northumberland.

No. of Div.	NAME.	TITLE.	ADDRESS.	COUNTY.
8	BEATTY, Thomas	M. D	*Etobicoke*	York.
11	BEAUBIEN, Jacques T. C	LCPS; L.C.	*Ottawa*	Carleton.
1	BEAUDET, Alfred	M. D	*Belle River*	Essex.
7	BEAUMONT, William R	FRCS; Eng	*Toronto*	York.
8	BEITH, Alex	M. B	*Bowmanville*	Durham.
9	BELL, Alex	M. D	*Lakefield, North Douro*	Peterboro'.
4	BELL, William	L. M. B	*Ayr*	Waterloo.
4	BENHAM, George	M. D	*Princeton*	Oxford.
8	BENSON, Edward	M. D	*Lindsay*	Victoria.
7	BENTLEY, John	M. D	*Newmarket*	York.
12	BERGIN, Darby	M. D	*Cornwall*	Stormont.
7	BERRYMAN, Charles Valance	M. D	*Yorkville*	York.
6	BETHUNE, Alex	M. D	*Glanford*	Wentworth.
9	BETHUNE, Alex. Norman	L. M. B	*Colborne*	Northumberland.
6	BETHUNE, Henry Fleming	M. D	*Glanford*	Wentworth.
1	BETTRIDGE, William	M. B	*Strathroy*	Middlesex.
1	BIGGAR, Geo. W	M. D	*Newbury*	Middlesex.
6	BIGGAR, Robert Henry	M. D	*Binbrook*	Wentworth.
8	BIGHAM, Hugh	M. D	*Hampton*	Durham.
8	BIGHAM, John	M. D	*Orono*	Durham.
6	BILLINGS, William Lockton	L. M. B	*Hamilton*	Wentworth.
1	BILLINGTON, George	LCPS; L.C.	*Strathroy*	Middlesex.
4	BINGHAM, Geo. Washington	M. D	*Ayr*	Waterloo.
8	BLACK, Wm. Anderson	M. D	*Omemee*	Victoria.
3	BLACKSTOCK, Wm. Harvey	M. D	*Hillsdale*	Simcoe.
5	BLACKWELL, Jno. Harrison	M. D	*Drummondville*	Welland.
4	BLAKE, Warren Hume	M. D	*Delhi*	Oxford.
2	BODDINGTON, George	M. D	*Sparta*	Elgin.
9	BOGART, Irvine Dorland	M. D	*Campbellford*	Northumberland.
4	BOGUE, Henry	M. D	*Haysville*	Waterloo.
8	BOLSTER, John	M. B	*Uxbridge*	Ontario.
8	BONNELL, Charles Edgar	M. D	*Bobcaygeon*	Victoria.
1	BOOK, James Burgess	M. D	*Windsor*	Essex.
10	BOOTH, Donald Bethune	M. D	*Odessa*	Addington.
9	BOULTER, Geo. Henry	M. D	*Stirling*	Hastings.
12	BOWER, Silas John	M. D	*Kemptville*	Grenville.
2	BOWIE, James	L. M. B	*Mitchell*	Perth.
4	BOWLBY, Alfred	M. D	*Waterford*	Norfolk.
3	BOWLBY, David Sovereign	M. D	*Berlin*	Wentworth;
5	BOWN, Edwin Theodore	M. D	*Brantford*	Brant.
5	BOWN, John Young	M. D	*Brantford*	Brant.
1	BOYD, Walter	M. D	*Arkona*	Lambton.
1	BOYLE, Arthur Richard	M. D	*Petrolea*	Lambton.
9	BRADLEY, Baldwin Lorenzo	M. D	*Stirling*	Hastings.
8	BRAITHWAITE, Fra's Horne	M. D	*Prince Albert*	Ontario.
6	BRANDON, John	M. D	*Ancaster*	Wentworth.
1	Bray, John Lang	M. D	*Chatham*	Kent.
9	BERETON, Charles Herbert	M. D	*Bethany*	Durham.
6	BRIDGEMAN, Irwin	M. D	*Stoney Creek*	Wentworth.
9	BRISTOL, Amos S	M. D	*Napanee*	Lennox.
7	BROCK, Llewellyn	M. D	*Toronto*	York.
12	BROUSE, William Henry	M. D	*Prescott*	Grenville.
4	BROWN, Brinton P	M. D	*Woodstock*	Oxford.
4	BROWN, Isaac Wesley	L. M. B	*Ingersoll*	Oxford.
7	BROWN, John	M. D	*Toronto*	York.
3	BROWN, John Price	M. B	*Hollen*	Wellington.
10	BROWN, Marshall J.	M. D	*Waterloo, K'n*	Frontenac.
2	BROWNING, Joseph William	M. D	*Exeter*	Huron.
7	BRUNSKILL, Thomas	M. D	*Bond Head*	Simcoe.
8	BRYSON, William Graham	M. D	*Fenelon Falls*	Victoria.
7	BUCHANAN, Chas. W., sen	M. D	*Toronto*	York.
7	BUCHANAN, Chas. W., jun	M. B	*Cookstown*	Simcoe.
7	BUCHANAN, Ogle R. Gowan	M. D	*Toronto*	York.
6	BUCK, Anson	M. D	*Palermo*	Halton.

No. of Div.	NAME.	TITLE.	ADDRESS.	COUNTY.
1	BUCKE, Richard Maurice...	M. D......	*Sarnia*	Lambton.
1	BUCKHAM, Thomas R......	M. D......	*Petrolea*	Lambton.
8	BULL, Edward............	L. M. B....	*Weston*	York.
6	BULLEN, Charles F........	M. D......	*Hamilton*	Wentworth.
10	BURDETT, David Earl......	M. B......	*Belleville*	Hastings.
5	BURGAR, William Edmund.	LRCPS; K'n	*Welland*	Welland.
9	BURNETT, David..........	M. B......	*Baltimore*	Northumberland.
3	BURNHAM, Elias La Fonta..	M. B	*Hillsburgh*	Wellington.
9	BURNHAM, George.........	L. M. B....	*Peterboro'*	Peterboro'.
9	BURNHAM, George.........	M. D......	*Ashburnham*	Peterboro'.
9	BURNHAM, Robert Wilkins..	M. D......	*Port Hope*	Durham.
7	BURNS, James Hepburn....	M. B......	*Toronto*	York.
9	BURRITT, Horatio Charles...	M. D.....	*Peterboro*	Peterboro.
11	BURRITT, Walter Horatio...	L. M. B....	*Smith's Falls*	Lanark.
9	BURROWS, Philip Palmer...	M. D......	*Millbrook*	Durham.
9	BUTLER, George Coltman...	M. D......	*Brighton*...............	Northumberland.
3	CAMERON, Allan..........	M. D......	*Owen Sound*..........	Grey.
9	CAMERON, Chas. McDonald.	M. D......	*Port Hope*	Durham.
6	CAMPBELL, D. Wolverton...	L. M. B....	*Stoney Creek*	Wentworth.
7	CAMPBELL, Duncan........	M. D......	*Toronto*	York.
12	CAMPBELL, Samuel........	M. D......	*Notfield*	Glengarry.
7	CANNIFF, William.........	M. D......	*Toronto*	York.
7	CARLYLE, James..........	M. D......	*Toronto*	York.
4	CARROLL, Daniel W........	M. D......	*Ingersoll*	Oxford.
4	CARROLL, James..........	L. M. B....	*Norwich*	Oxford.
8	CARSON, George Alva......	M. D......	*Whitby*	Ontario.
2	CASCADEN, John..........	M. B......	*Iona*	Elgin.
6	CASE, William I. A.......	L. M. B....	*Hamilton*	Wentworth.
1	CASGRAIN, Charles Eugene.	M. D......	*Windsor*	Essex.
3	CASSADY, John Francis....	M. D......	*Walkerton*	Bruce.
2	CATTERMOLE, James.......	M. D......	*London*	Middlesex.
1	CAW, William............	M. D......	*Park Hill*	Middlesex.
5	CHAMBERLAIN, Aaron H....	M. D......	*Kelvin*	Brant.
1	CHAMBERLAIN, Charles.....	M. D......	*Leamington*	Essex.
12	CHAMBERLAIN, Theodore F..	M. D......	*Morrisburg*	Dundas.
9	CHAMBERLAIN, Thomas.....	L. M. B....	*Napanee*	Lennox.
7	CHEWETT, William Cameron	M. D......	*Toronto*	York.
5	CHRISTIE, John Boyd......	M. D......	*Brantford*	Brant.
3	CHRISTOE, William S.....	M. D......	*Flesherton*	Grey.
5	CRYSLER, William Henry...	M. B......	*Burford*	Brant.
11	CHURCH, Clarence Ronald..	M. D......	*Ashton.*	Carleton.
12	CHURCH, Mills Kemble.....	M. D......	*Merrickville*	Grenville.
4	CLARKE, Daniel...........	M. D......	*Princeton*	Oxford.
4	CLARKE, John............	L. M. B....	*Simcoe*	Norfolk.
12	CLARKE, Robert Caldwell...	LFPS; Glas	*L'Orignal*	Prescott.
3	CLARKE, William.........	LRCS; Irel.	*Guelph*	Wellington.
5	CLARKE, William..........	L. M. B....	*Paris*	Brant.
10	CLARK, James Farley......	M. D......	*Bloomfield*	Prince Edward.
7	CLEMENT, Lewis..........	M. D......	*Bradford*	Simcoe.
9	CLEMESHA, John W........	M. D......	*Port Hope*............	Durham.
8	CLOSSON, Lorenzo.........	L. M. B....	*Woburn*..............	York.
4	COAD, John Foote.........	MRCS; Eng	*East Zorra, Woodstock, P. O.*............	Oxford.
8	COBURN, William.........	M. D......	*Oshawa*	Ontario.
11	CODD, Alfred............	M. D......	*Ottawa.*	Carleton.
8	COGAN, Jerimiah R........	M. D......	*Lindsay*	Victoria.
2	COLE, Henry William......	M. B	*Clinton*	Huron.
10	COLEMAN, Everett Hastings.	L. M. B....	*Belleville.*	Hastings.
2	COLEMAN, Timothy T......	L. M. B....	*Seaforth*	Huron.
12	COLEMAN, Wm. Franklin...	M. D......	*Lyn*	Leeds.
4	COLLVER, Addison J.......	M. D......	*Otterville*	Oxford.
4	COLLVER, John G.........	M. D......	*Waterford*.	Norfolk.
10	COLTON, Wm. Wallace.....	M. D......	*Consecon*........	Prince Edward.
5	COMFORT, John Harris.....	M. D......	*St. Catharines*	Lincoln.

64

No. of Div.	NAME.	TITLE.	ADDRESS.	COUNTY.
5	Comfort, William A	M. D......	*Beamsville*	Lincoln.
7	Constantinides, Petros	M. D......	*Toronto*	York.
5	Cook, Alex. Hardy	M. D......	*Mount Pleasant, Mohawk P. O.*	Brant.
4	Cook, Ephraim	L. M. B	*Norwich*	Oxford.
3	Cooke, George	M. D......	*Ederslie, Scone P.O.*	Bruce.
11	Cooke, Sidney P..........	M. D......	*Ottawa*	Carleton.
5	Cooke, Silas Wright	L. M. B	*Paris*	Brant.
9	Cook, Hermon Levi	M. D......	*Brighton*	Northumberland.
3	Corbett, George Henry....	M. D......	*Orillia*	Simcoe.
9	Corbett, Robert A........	M. D......	*Perrytown*	Durham.
9	Corbett, Samuel Charles..	M. D......	*Perrytown*	Durham.
6	Cornwall, Vincent C......	M. D......	*West Flamboro'*	Wentworth.
5	Corry, Matthew Nixon....	M. D......	*Stamford*	Welland.
4	Corson, John.............	M. D......	*Washington*	Oxford.
5	Corson, William Case.....	M. D......	*Brantford*	Brant.
9	Coulter, Charles L........	M. D......	*Peterboro'*	Peterboro'.
1	Couse, George............	M. D......	*Wardsville*	Middlesex. ✓
1	Coventry, John	M. D......	*Wardsville*	Middlesex. ✓
4	Covernton, Charles Wm...	M. D......	*Simcoe*	Norfolk.
3	Cowan, James............	M. D......	*Harriston*	Wellington.
1	Cowan, Richard...........	MRCS; Eng	*Strathroy*	Middlesex.
11	Cowan, Samuel............	M. B......	*Nanotick*	Carleton.
3	Crandall, Byron..........	M. D......	*Clifford*	Wellington.
11	Cranston, James G........	M. D......	*Arnprior*	Renfrew.
3	Crawford, Joseph.........	M. D......	*Durham*	Grey.
6	Crooker, Titus............	M. D......	*Hamilton*	Wentworth.
3	Crookshank, Jas. Stewart..	LFPS; Glas	*Barrie*	Simcoe.
5	Cross, Luther............	L. M. B	*St. Catharines*	Lincoln.
6	Crumbie, John............	M. D......	*Streetsville*	Peel.
6	Currey, Reuben Chapman.	M. D......	*Brampton*	Peel.
6	Dalton, William Henry...	LCPS; U.C.	*Bolton Village*	Peel.
10	Darragh, Robert James....	M. D......	*Kingston*	Frontenac.
8	Davidson, Jackson Graham.	M. D......	*Bowmanville*..	Durham.
5	Davis, Robert Henry	M. D......	*York*	Haldimand.
1	Davison, Myers...........	M. D......	*Florence*	Lambton.
8	Davison, Peter............	M. D......	*Beaverton*	Ontario.
9	Davison, Solomon Wright.	L. M. B	*Baillieboro*	Durham.
10	Day, Barnabus W..........	M. D......	*Kingston*	Frontenac.
10	Day, Henry W............	M. D......	*Trenton*	Hastings.
9	Dean, Marshall Pulaski....	M. D......	*Keene*	Peterboro.
9	Dean, Noble Benjamin....	M. D......	*Brighton*	Northumberland.
10	Deans, George	M. D......	*Trenton*	Hastings.
4	Deans, Wm Carter........	M. D......	*Galt*	Waterloo.
5	Dee, Robert Hill..........	M. D......	*Middleport*	Brant.
8	De Grassi, Alex. Wm. Jas.	M. D......	*Oakwood*	Victoria.
7	De Grassi, Geo. Philip....	M. B......	*Toronto*	York.
8	De la Haye, Alcide J. B. G.	M. B......	*Clairville, Humber, P.O.*	York.
7	De la Hooke, Jas. Ackland	MRCS; Eng	*Toronto*	York.
9	Demorest, Burnham G. G..	M. D......	*Norham*	Northumberland.
8	D'Evelyn, John	M. D......	*Woodbridge*	York.
9	Dewar, John Forrest......	M. D......	*Port Hope*	Durham.
12	Dickinson, George........	M. D... ..	*Russell*	Russell.
12	Dickinson, James John....	M. D......	*Cornwall*	Stormont.
10	Dickson, John Robinson...	M. D......	*Kingston*............	Frontenac.
5	Dickson, James W. R.....	LRCS.; Ed.	*Paris*	Brant.
11	Dickson, Wm. Welland....	M. D......	*Pembroke*	Lanark.
5	Digby, Winnlett...........	M. D......	*Brantford*	Brant.
5	Dillabough, Edmund H'y..	L. M. B	*Caledonia*	Haldimand.
6	Dixie, Beaumont W.B.....	L. M. B	*Springfield, Credit*.....	Peel.
8	Dodd, John...............	M. D......	*Newcastle*............	Durham.
1	Donnelly, Edmund Burke.	L. M. B	*Windsor*............	Essex.
10	Dorland, Peter Van Buren.	M. D......	*Belleville*	Hastings.
6	Douglas, Charles	M. B......	*Streetsville*	Peel.

No. of Div.	NAME.	TITLE.	ADDRESS.	COUNTY.
1	DOUGLAS, James	M. D	*Chatham*	Kent.
3	DOUGLASS, Robert	M. D	*Normanton*	Bruce.
5	DOWNEY, William S	M. D	*St. Catharines*	Lincoln.
1	DRAKE, William H	M. D	*Kingsville*	Essex.
6	DUGGAN, Thomas	L. M. B	*Hamilton*	Wentworth.
11	DUHAMEL, Louis	M. D	*Pembroke*	Renfrew.
3	DUNBAR, Samuel	M. D	*Mount Forest*	Wellington.
4	DUNCOMB, David	L. M. B	*Waterford*	Norfolk.
4	DUNCOMBE, Alex. C	M. D	*Boston*	Norfolk.
12	DUNHAM, George	M. D	*Newboro*	Leeds.
12	DUNN, Andrew Thomas	M. D	*North Agusta*	Grenville.
10	DUPUIS, Thomas R	M. D	*Odessa*	Addington.
12	EASTON, John	M. D	*Prescott*	Grenville.
7	EASTWOOD, Charles S	M. D	*Toronto*	York.
8	EASTWOOD, William O	M. D	*Whitby*	Ontario.
2	EBY, Aaron	M. D	*Sebringville*	Perth.
1	ECCLES, Fra's Richard	M. D	*Arkona*	Lambton.
3	ECROYD, Alfred E	MRCS; Eng	*Mount Forest*	Wellington.
12	EDMONDSON, Robert	M. D	*Brockville*	Leeds.
1	EDWARDS, Eliphalet G	M. D	*Strathroy*	Middlesex.
9	ELMER, William W	M. D	*Madoc*	Hastings.
8	EMERY, Gordon Jas	M. D	*Bowmanville*	Durham.
7	EMERY, Robert	M. D	*Toronto*	York.
3	EMES, Silas P	M. D	*Drayton*	Wellington.
9	ENGLISH, Timothy F	M. D	*Stirling*	Hastings.
10	EVANS, Henry B	MRCS; Eng	*Picton*	Prince Edward.
9	EVATT, William Henry	M. D	*Port Hope*	Durham.
8	FAIR, Robert C	M. D	*Bobcaygeon*	Victoria.
12	FALKNER, Alexander	M. D	*New Lancaster, Riviere Raisin*	Glengarry.
5	FARES, Owen Wm	M. D	*Port Colborne*	Welland.
5	FARRELL, John T	M. D	*Dunnville*	Haldimand.
10	FEE, Samuel H	M. D	*Kingston*	Frontenac.
10	FENWICK, Thomas N	M. D	*Kingston*	Frontenac.
1	FERGUSSON, John	M. D	*Chatham*	Kent.
11	FERGUSSON, Robert B	M. D	*Lanark*	Lanark.
8	FERRIER, David Wm	M. D	*Brougham*	Ontario.
8	FIDLER, Joshua	L. M. B	*Lindsay*	Victoria.
6	FIFE, Joseph A	M. D	*Brampton*	Peel.
10	FILE, Albert John	M. D	*Lonsdale*	Hastings.
1	FISHER, Andrew	L. M. B	*Amherstburg*	Essex.
7	FISHER Edward John T	M. D	*Bradford*	Simcoe.
8	FITZGERALD, James	M. D	*Fenelon Falls*	Victoria.
2	FITZSIMMONS, George	M. D	*Egmondville*	Huron.
4	FLEAK, Henry C	M. D	*Ingersoll*	Oxford.
6	FLOCK, Christopher W	M. D	*Freelton*	Wentworth.
2	FLYNN, John	L. M. B	*Shakespeare*	Perth.
2	FOOTE, Ezra	L. M. B	*Aylmer*	Elgin.
11	FORBES, George	M. D	*Beachburg*	Renfrew.
5	FORBES, John	LRCS.; Ed.	*Chippawa*	Welland.
7	FORREST, Robert Wilson	L. M. B	*Mount Albert*	York.
2	FORSTER, Moffit	M. D	*Thorndale*	Middlesex.
10	FOWLER, Fife	M. D	*Kingston*	Frontenac.
9	FOWLER, Robert	M. D	*Colborne*	Northumberland.
1	FRANCIS, Abraham	MRCS; Eng	*Delaware*	Middlesex.
3	FRANCIS, William S	M. B	*Invermay*	Bruce.
4	FRANKLIN, Benjamin	M. D	*Pleasant Hill*	Norfolk.
1	FRASER, Anson S	M. D	*Wallaceburg*	Kent.
2	FRASER, John M	M. D	*London*	Middlesex.
5	FRAZER, John	L. M. B	*Fonthill*	Welland.
7	FREEL, Sylvester L	Cer. T. S. M.	*Stouffville*	York.
6	FREEMAN, Clarkson	M. D	*Milton*	Halton.
6	FREEMAN, William	M. D	*Georgetown*	Halton.
2	FULTON, John	M. D	*Fingal*	Elgin.

No. of Div.	NAME.	TITLE.	ADDRESS.	COUNTY.
2	Gairdner, Robert H	M. D	*Bayfield*	Huron.
1	Gamble, Aaron W	M. D	*Moore*	Lambton.
11	Garvey, Joseph	M. D	*Ottawa*	Carleton.
2	Gates, Edward Henry	M. D	*Vienna*	Elgin. ✓
7	Geikie, Walter B	M. D	*Aurora*	York.
3	Ghent, Byron E	M. D	*Priceville*	Grey.
1	Gibson, Edward	M. D	*Hillsboro*	Lambton.
11	Gibson, Edward B	M. D	*Pakenham*	Lanark.
9	Gilchrist, James A	L. M. B	*Cobourg*	Northumberland.
12	Giles, John G	M. D	*Farmersville*	Leeds.
3	Gilmore, William R	M. B	*Penetanguishene*	Simcoe.
8	Gillespie, Donald	M. D	*Cannington*	Ontario.
5	Goforth, Franklin	M. D	*Stevensville*	Welland.
2	Going, Frederick B	LRCS.; Irel	*St. Thomas*	Elgin. ✓
5	Goodman, Edwin	M. B	*St. Catharines*	Lincoln.
12	Gordon, Hugh Alex	M. D	*Brockville*	Leeds.
2	Gowans, Robert	M. D	*Shakespeare*	Perth.
2	Graham, William	M. D	*Ainleyville, Dingle P. O.*	Huron.
9	Grange, James	M. D	*Napanee*	Lennox.
12	Grant, Donald J	M. D	*Winchester*	Dundas.
11	Grant, James A	M. D	*Ottawa*	Carleton.
6	Grant, John	L. M. B	*Brampton*	Peel.
11	Grant, William	M. D	*Perth*	Lanark.
1	Grasse, Sidney D	M. D	*Windsor*	Essex.
5	Griffin, Egerton	M. D	*Brantford*	Brant.
3	Gun, James	M. D	*Durham*	Grey.
8	Gunn, Robert John	LRCS.; Ed.	*Whitby*	Ontario. ✓
2	Gustin, Eliphalet W	M. D	*St. Thomas*	Elgin. ✓
7	Hackett, James	L.M.B	*Newmarket*	York.
2	Hagerty, Daniel	M. D	*London*	Middlesex. ✓
4	Hagerman, Wm. Charles	M. D	*Lynedoch*	Norfolk.
12	Haight, Edward Benjamin	M. D	*Mallorytown*	Leeds.
7	Hall, Cyrenius B	M. D	*Toronto*	York.
12	Hall, John Dow	LRCPS; K'n	*Brockville*	Leeds.
9	Halliday, James T. I	M. D	*Vernonville*	Northumberland.
7	Hallowell, William	M. D	*Toronto*	York.
3	Hamilton, Alex	M. D	*Barrie*	Simcoe.
10	Hamilton, Charles S	M. D	*Lonsdale*	Hastings.
6	Hamilton, James	LRCS.; Ed.	*Dundas*	Wentworth.
6	Hamilton, John M	LRCS.; Ed.	*Hamilton*	Wentworth.
7	Hampton, William B	L.M.B	*Toronto*	York.
2	Hanavan, M. J	M. B	*Stratford*	Perth.
5	Haney, Matthew F	L.M. B	*Humberstone*	Welland.
5	Haney, Robert A	M. D	*Caistorville*	Lincoln.
2	Hanvey, William Henry	L.M.B	*Stratford*	Perth.
5	Harbottle, Robert	M.B	*Burford*	Brant.
12	Harkin, William	M. D	*Vankleek Hill*	Prescott.
2	Harper, Alfred	M. D	*London*	Middlesex. ✓
2	Harrison, David. H	M. D	*St. Marys*	Perth.
5	Harrison, Thomas T. S	M. D	*Selkirk*	Haldimand.
9	Harvey, Alex	M. D	*Peterboro'*	Peterboro'
3	Harvey, Samuel A	L.M.B	*Glenallen*	Wellington.
4	Hayes, James	M. D	*Simcoe*	Norfolk.
6	Heggie, David	M. D	*Brampton*	Peel.
3	Henderson, Donald	M. D	*Ailsa Craig*	Middlesex. ✓
3	Henry, James	M. D	*Orangeville*	Wellington.
11	Henry, Walter Jas	M. D	*Ottawa*	Carleton.
6	Henwood, Edwin	L.M.B	*Hamilton*	Wentworth.
5	Henwood, Reginald	L.M.B	*Brantford*	Brant.
3	Herod, George S	L.M.B	*Guelph*	Wellington.
8	Herriman, E. A	M. D	*Lindsay*	Victoria.
8	Herriman, W. L	M. D	*Orono*	Durham.
3	Hewat, William S	MRCS; Eng	*Orangeville*	Wellington.
12	Hickey, Charles E	M. D	*West Winchester*	Dundas.

[illegible] of [illegible]	NAME.	TITLE.	ADDRESS.	COUNTY.
2	HICKEY, Rueben I........	M. D......	*Aultsville*............	Dundas.
6	HICKMAN, Edward.........	MRCS; Eng	*Bolton Village*.........	Peel.
9	HIGINBOTHAM, Andrew.....	LRCPS; K'n	*Bridgewater*..........	Hastings.
3	HILL, Alexander.........	M. D......	*Teviotdale*..........	Wellington.
11	HILL, Hamnett...........	MRCS; Eng	*Ottawa*............	Carleton.
8	HILLARY, James J........	L.M.B ...	*Uxbridge*............	Ontario.
7	HILLARY, Robert Wm......	L.M.B	*Aurora*............	York.
5	HIPKINS, Edward.........	L.M.B	*Burford*............	Brant.
1	HOARE, Walter W.........	M. D......	*Adelaide*............	Middlesex. ✓
7	HODDER, Edward M........	FRCS; Eng	*Toronto*............	York.
10	HOLDEN, Rufus...........	M. D......	*Belleville*............	Hastings.
1	HOLMES, T. K............	M. D......	*Chatham*............	Kent.
2	HOLMES, William J. R....	M. D......	*Dingle*............	Huron.
10	HOPE, William..........	M. D......	*Belleville*............	Hastings.
2	HORNIBROOK, Edward	M. D......	*Mitchell*............	Perth.
11	HORSEY, Edward H.......	M. D......	*Perth*............	Lanark.
8	HOSTETTER, John.........	MRCS; Eng	*Richmond Hill*.........	York.
11	HOWDEN, Robert..........	M. D......	*Perth*............	Lanark.
6	HOWE, Thomas Charles....	M. B......	*Dundas*............	Wentworth.
5	HOWELL, William Allan...	M. D......	*Jarvis*............	Haldimand.
5	HOWELLS, Thomas B.......	M. D......	*Caledonia*............	Haldimand.
3	HOWITT, John	M. D......	*Guelph*............	Wellington.
4	HOWLAND, Fra's L........	M. D......	*Woodstock*............	Oxford.
7	HOWSON, Joseph..........	L.M.B	*Toronto*............	York.
4	HOYT, John J............	M. D......	*Ingersoll*............	Oxford.
3	HUGHES, Samuel Lount....	M. D......	*Berlin*............	Waterloo.
7	HUNTER, James J.........	M. D......	*Newmarket*............	York.
3	HURLBURT, George W......	M. D......	*Thornbury*............	Grey.
1	HUTTON, James...........	M. D......	*Farrest*............	Lambton.
2	HYDE, John..............	LFPS; Glas	*Stratford*............	Perth.
2	HYNDMAND, John..........	L.M.B	*Exeter*............	Huron.
12	IMESON, Archibald.......	M. D......	*Delta*............	Leeds.
8	INGERSOLL, Isaac F......	M. D......	*Lindsay*............	Victoria.
10	IRWIN, Chamberlain A....	M. D......	*Wolfe Island*.........	Frontenac.
11	IRWIN, James............	MRCS; Eng	*Pembroke*............	Lanark.
7	JACKES, Albert G........	M. B......	*Toronto*............	York.
2	JACKSON, John P.........	M. B......	*Stratford*............	Perth.
5	JARRON, John	LRCS.; Ed.	*Dunnville*............	Haldimand.
4	JARVIS, Joseph..........	M. D......	*Ingersoll*............	Oxford.
10	JOHNSON, A. H...........	M. D.	*Portsmouth*............	Frontenac.
2	JOHNSON, James..........	M. D......	*Millbank*............	Perth.
5	JOHNSTON, Robert James...	M. B......	*Thorold*............	Welland.
1	JOHNSTON, Thomas Wm....	L.M.B	*Sarnia*............	Lambton.
7	JOLLEY, John............	M. D....	*Alliston*............	Simcoe.
3	JONES, Charles A........	M. D......	*Rockwood*............	Wellington.
7	JONES, Charles B........	M. D......	*Toronto*............	York.
8	JONES, George W.........	M. D......	*Prince Albert*.........	Ontario.
5	JONES, Peter Edmund.....	M. D......	*Niagara*............	Lincoln.
12	JONES, William J........	M. D......	*Prescott*............	Grenville.
4	JOY, Sylvanus...........	M. D......	*Woodstock*............	Oxford.
5	JUKES, Augustus.........	M. B......	*St. Catharines*.........	Lincoln.
6	KEAGEY, David...........	M. D......	*Hamilton*............	Wentworth.
3	KEATING, Thomas A.......	M. D......	*Guelph*............	Wellington.
11	KELLOCK, John Dickson ...	M. D......	*Perth*............	Lanark.
1	KEMP, James A...........	M. D......	*Leamington*............	Essex.
5	KEMPSON, P. Tertius......	MRCS; Eng	*Fort Erie*............	Welland.
8	KEMPT, William..........	M. D......	*Lindsay*............	Victoria.
3	KENNEDY, James..........	L. M. B....	*Chatsworth*............	Grey.
7	KENNEDY, John E.........	M. B......	*Toronto*............	York.
10	KENNEDY, Roderick.......	M. D......	*Bath*............	Addington.
3	KERR, Bernard S.........	M. D......	*Maxwell*............	Grey.
4	KERR, William...........	LFPS; Glas	*Galt*............	Waterloo.
11	KERTLAND, Edwin H.......	M. D......	*Pakenham*............	Lanark.
9	KINCAID, Robert.........	M. D......	*Peterboro'*............	Peterboro'

No. of Div.	NAME.	TITLE.	ADDRESS.	COUNTY.
7	KING, John L.	M. B.	*Toronto*	York.
10	KING, Richard	M. D.	*Bloomfield*	Prince Edward.
1	KING, Sindey A.	M. D.	*Kingsville*	Essex.
5	KIRK, John	L. M. B.	*Canboro'*	Haldimand.
5	KITCHEN, Edward E.	M. B.	*St. George*	Brant.
8	KNOWLYS, Culling E.	M. D.	*Greenbank*	Ontario.
4	KOETSCH, Earnest A.	L. M. B.	*Preston*	Waterloo.
6	LAING, James B.	M. D.	*Hamilton*	Wentworth.
1	LAMBERT, Robert	M. D.	*Windsor*	Essex.
1	LAMBERT, Walter	M. B.	*Amherstburg*	Essex.
3	LANDERKIN, George	M. D.	*Hanover*	Grey.
1	LANDOR, Henry	MRCS; Eng	*Amherstburg*	Essex.
5	LANE, William	M. D.	*St. Catharines*	Lincoln.
3	LA[illegible]G, Thomas D.	M. D.	*Owen Sound*	Grey.
5	LANGRILL, John A.	M. B.	*Jarvis*	Haldimand.
8	LANGSTAFF, James	L. M. B.	*Richmond Hill*	York.
7	LANGSTAFF, Lewis	M. D.	*King*	York.
8	LAPS[illegible]EY, William	L. M. B.	*Woburn*	York.
10	LAVELL, Michael	M. D.	*Kingston*	Frontenac
3	LAW, William D. C.	M. D.	*Heathcote*	Grey.
8	LAW, William Henry	M. D.	*Bowmanville*	Durham.
7	LAWLOR, Michael	M. D.	*Toronto*	York.
5	LAWRENCE, John	L. M. B.	*Paris*	Brant.
11	LEGGO, Christopher	L. M. B.	*Ottawa*	Carleton.
5	LEMON, Benjamin H.	M. D.	*Thorold*	Welland.
9	LEWIS, Richard P.	M. B.	*Perrytown*	Durham.
3	LIGHTBODY, John	L. M. B.	*Douglas*	Wellington.
2	LINO, George W.	M. D.	*Tempo*	Middlesex.
10	LISTER, James	M. D.	*Belleville*	Hastings.
7	LIZARS, John L.	MRCS; Eng	*Toronto*	York.
7	LLOYD, Rolph C.	M. D.	*Stouffville*	York.
3	LOUNT, Gabriel	M. D.	*Hawkesville*	Waterloo.
7	LUND, Richard	M. D.	*Cookstown*	Simcoe.
6	LUNDY, John B.	M. D.	*Sheffield*	Wentworth.
1	LUNDY, William C.	M. D.	*Amherstburg*	Essex.
6	LUSK, Charles H.	M. D.	*Oakville*	Halton.
3	LUTZ, Calvin	M. D.	*Glen Allan*	Wellington.
5	MACK, Francis L.	M. D.	*St. Catharines*	Lincoln.
5	MACK, Theophilus	M. D.	*St. Catharines*	Lincoln.
7	MADILL, John	M. D.	*Alliston*	Simcoe.
7	MAHAFFY, John	MRCS; Eng	*Nobleton*	York.
7	MALCOLM, John R.	M. D.	*Toronto*	York.
6	MALLOCH, Archibald	M. B.	*Hamilton*	Wentworth.
11	MALLOCH, Edward C.	M. D.	*Ottawa*	Carleton.
3	MANLEY, Henry	MRCS; Eng	*Owen Sound*	Grey.
2	MANN, Peregrine, M.	M. D.	*Bayham*	Elgin.
6	MANWARING, N. E.	M. D.	*St. George*	Brant.
1	MARK, Robert	M. D.	*Wallaceburg*	Kent.
12	MARKELL, Richard S.	M. D.	*Osnabruck Centre*	Stormont.
6	MARLATT, Jonathan W.	M. D.	*Ontario*	Wentworth.
5	MARQUIS, Duncan	M. D.	*Mohawk*	Brant.
9	MARTEN, Henry Oake	L. M. B.	*Colborne*	Northumberland.
8	MARTIN, Caleb E.	M. D.	*Lindsay*	Victoria.
3	MARTYN, DeWitt Harry	M. D.	*Kincardine*	Bruce.
4	MASSECAR, A. J.	M. D.	*Otterville*	Oxford.
9	MASSIE, John	M. D.	*Colborne*	Northumberland.
3	MAUDESLEY, Henry	M. D.	*Hollen*	Wellington.
10	MEAGHER, James	L. M. B.	*Kingston*	Frontenac.
2	MERCER, John F.	M. D.	*Goderich*	Huron.
2	METHERELL, George W.	M. D.	*Seaforth*	Huron.
5	MEWBURN, Francis C.	M. D.	*Drummondville*	Welland.
3	MIDDLETON, William G.	L. M. B.	*Elora*	Wellington.
9	MIGHT, James	M. D.	*Millbrook*	Durham.
3	MILLER, Allan H.	M. D.	*Mount Forest*	Wellington.

No. of Div.	NAME.	TITLE.	ADDRESS.	COUNTY.
6	MILLER, Samuel	L. M. B.	*Hamilton*	Wentworth.
6	MILLER, Thomas	M. D.	*West Flamboro'*	Wentworth.
4	MILLER, William Henry	M. B.	*Port Dover*	Norfolk.
2	MILLS, John B.	M. D.	*Springfield*	Elgin.
5	MILLWARD, Wm. Edward	M. D.	*Grimsby*	Lincoln.
7	MINGAYE, Charles P	MRCS; Eng	*Toronto*	York.
2	MITCHELL, David	M. D.	*Iona*	Elgin.
1	MITCHELL, George	Cer.T.S.M.	*Wallaceburg*	Kent.
3	MOBERLY, Arthur	L. M. B.	*Stayner*	Simcoe.
12	MONGENAIS, Napoleon	LCPS; L.C.	*St. Eugene*	Prescott.
8	MONTGOMERY, John	M. B.	*Cartwright*	Durham.
11	MOORE, Andrew	M. D.	*Renfrew*	Renfrew.
9	MOORE, Charles C.	MRCS; Eng	*Cobourg*	Northumberland.
2	MOORE, Samuel	M. D.	*Nilestown*	Middlesex.
10	MOORE, Thomas	L. M. B.	*Picton*	Prince Edward.
10	MORDEN, James B.	M. D.	*Picton*	Prince Edward.
12	MORDEN, John H.	M. D.	*Brockville*	Leeds.
8	MORGAN, John Thos.	MRCS; Eng	*Bobcaygeon*	Victoria.
1	MORRIS, William	LRCS; Irel.	*Delaware*	Middlesex.
4	MORRISON, John S.	L. M. B.	*Plattsville*	Oxford.
6	MORROW, Robert.	M. D.	*Acton*	Halton.
5	MORSON, Frederick	MRCS; Eng	*Niagara*	Lincoln
7	MORTON, Edward	M. D	*Queensville*	York.
3	MORTON, Edward D.	M. B.	*Barrie*	Simcoe.
7	MORTON, George D.	L. M. B.	*Bradford*	Simcoe.
3	MORTON, William	M. B.	*Wellesley*	Waterloo.
11	MOSTYN, William	M. D.	*Almonte*	Lanark.
1	MOTHERSILL, Joseph	L. M. B.	*Arkona*	Lambton.
6	MULLIN, John A.	M. D.	*Hamilton*	Wentworth.
6	MULLIN, John T.	M. D.	*Tullamore*	Peel.
3	MULLOY, Nelson	M. D.	*Doon*	Waterloo.
1	MUNNS, William A.	M. D.	*Widder*	Lambton.
11	MUNRO, David	M. D.	*Lanark*	Lanark.
3	MUNRO, John	LRCS.; Ed.	*Fergus*	Wellington.
2	MUNRO, Neil	M. D.	*Brucefield*	Huron.
1	MURPHY, Henry Joseph	M. D.	*Chatham*	Kent.
2	MUTER, Peter J.	M. D.	*Shakespeare*	Perth.
11	MACDONALD, Æneas	LCPS; L.C.	*Ottawa*	Carleton.
12	MACDONALD, Angus.	M. D.	*Cornwall*	Stormont.
6	MACDONALD, John Duff	M. D.	*Hamilton*	Wentworth.
1	MACINTYRE, Duncan	M. D.	*Wardsville*	Middlesex.
4	MACKAY, Hugh M	M. D.	*Woodstock*	Oxford.
6	MACKAY, James Angus	L. M. B.	*Castlemore*	Peel.
6	MACKELCAN, George Lloyd.	M. D.	*Hamilton*	Wentworth.
6	MACKELCAN, John	MRCS; Eng	*Hamilton*	Wentworth.
3	MACKERACHER, Alexander	M. D.	*Duntroon*	Simcoe.
3	MACKINNON, Angus	M. D.	*Ailsa Craig*	Middlesex.
6	MACKINTOSH, David	M. D.	*Hamilton*	Wentworth.
3	MACLEAN, Caird Ryerson	M. D.	*Meaford*	Grey.
10	MACLEAN, Donald	M. D.	*Kingston*	Frontenac.
1	MACKLEM, Samuel Street	M. D.	*Oil Springs*	Lambton.
6	MACRAE, Charles A.	M. D.	*Lynden*	Wentworth.
1	MCALPINE, Dugald Leitch	M. B.	*Glencoe*	Middlesex.
1	MCALPINE, Robert Smith	Cer. T. S. M.	*Petrolea*	Lambton.
5	MCCALLUM, George A.	M. D.	*Dunnville*	Haldimand.
4	MCCALLUM, James	M. B.	*Culloden*	Oxford.
10	MCCAMMON, James	M. D.	*Newburg*	Addington.
1	MCCANDLESS, Francis	M. D.	*Falkirk*	Middlesex.
5	MCCARGOW, William	LFPS; Glas	*Caledonia*	Haldimand.
7	MCCARTHY, John L. G	M. B.	*Bradford*	Simcoe.
4	MCCAUSLAND, Marshall B.	M. D.	*Ingersoll*	Oxford.
8	MCCAUSLAND, Thomas	L. M. B.	*Markham*	York.
8	MCCLINTON, Nathaniel	M. D	*Sonya*	Ontario.
2	MCCOOL, Daniel Brown	M. B.	*Dingle P.O., Ainleyville*	Huron.

No. of Div.	NAME.	TITLE.	ADDRESS.	COUNTY.
9	McCrea, Amos	L. M. B	*Keene*	Peterboro'.
9	McCrea, James Nelson	M. D	*Wakworth*	Northumberland.
1	McCulley, Samuel Edward	M. D	*Chatham*	Kent.
3	McCullough, James	M. B	*Everton*	Wellington.
9	McCullough, John Rob't	L. M. B	*Peterboro'*	Peterboro'.
12	McDiarmid, Donald	M. D	*Athol*	Glengarry.
8	McDiarmid, Peter	M.B	*Malvern*	York.
4	McDonald, Samuel	M. D	*Cullodon*	Oxford.
2	McDougall, Peter	M. D	*Goderich*	Huron.
11	McDougall, Peter Alex	M. D	*Osgoode*	Carleton.
5	McFarland, Jno. Cameron	LCPS; L.C.	*Port Robinson*	Welland.
5	McGarry, James	M. D	*Drummondville*	Welland.
6	McGarvin, Nelson	M. D	*Acton*	Halton.
1	McGeachy, William	M. D	*Chatham*	Kent.
8	McGill William	M. D	*Oshawa*	Ontario.
11	McGillivray, Donald	M. D	*Ottawa*	Carleton.
3	McGregor, Duncan	M. D	*Chatsworth*	Grey.
3	McGregor, James Henry	M. D	*Guelph*	Wellington.
6	McGregor, William	M. D	*Cummingsville*	Halton.
3	McGuire, Edward William	M. D	*Guelph*	Wellington.
7	McIlmurray, James	MRCS; Eng	*Toronto*	York.
1	McInnes, Loftus Robert	M. D	*Newbury*	Middlesex.
4	McInnes, Walter J. M	M. D	*Vittoria*	Norfolk.
3	McIntosh, Robert	M. D	*Meaford*	Grey.
1	McIntyre, David Cameron	M. D	*Glencoe*	Middlesex.
9	McIntyre, Neil	M. B	*Janetville*	Durham.
3	McIntyre, Robert	M. D	*Hespeler*	Waterloo.
8	McKay, Alexander	M. D	*Beaverton*	Ontario.
7	McKay, William	M. B	*Churchill*	Simcoe.
1	McKellar, Dugald S	M. D	*Strathroy*	Middlesex.
11	McKenzie, Andrew	M. D	*Ottawa*	Carleton.
11	McKenzie, Edward	M. D	*Pembroke*	Renfrew.
12	McKinnon, Hugh D	Cer. T. S. M	*St. Eugene*	Prescott.
12	McLaren, Alexander	M. D	*Riceville*	Prescott.
3	McLaren, Peter	M. D	*Paisley*	Bruce.
2	McLaughlin, James	M. D	*Fingal*	Elgin.
8	McLaughlin, James W	M. B	*Enniskillen*	Durham.
1	McLean, Archibald	M. D	*Sarnia*	Lambton.
2	McLean, Thomas F	M. D	*Goderich*	Huron.
1	McLeay, John Dougald	Cer. T. S. M	*Lobo*	Middlesex.
4	McLeod, Hugh	M. D	*Harrington*	Oxford.
6	McMahon, James	L. M. B	*Dundas*	Wentworth.
3	McManus, George Carson	M. D.	*Creemore*	Simcoe.
2	McMicking, George M	M. D	*Goderich*	Huron.
12	McMillan, Donald	M. D	*Alexandria*	Glengarry.
2	McMurchie, Duncan Wm	M. D	*Clinton*	Huron.
9	McNabb, John	LRCS.; Ed.	*Peterboro'*	Peterboro'.
1	McTaggart, Alexander	M. D	*Strathroy*	Middlesex.
2	McTavish, Archibald	M. D	*Staffa*	Perth.
11	McVean, John	M. D	*Carleton Place*	Lanark.
1	Nash, Hutchison James	L. M. B	*Warwick*	Lambton.
10	Nash, Samuel L	M. D	*Ameliasburgh*	Prince Edward.
8	Nation, John	L. M. B	*Uxbridge*	Ontario.
2	Nelles, John A	M. D	*London*	Middlesex.
3	Nesbitt, Edward	M. D	*Huston*	Wellington.
7	Newcombe, James	M. D	*Toronto*	York.
7	Newcombe, William	M. D	*Toronto*	York.
1	Newman, John Byron	M. B	*Wallaceburg*	Kent.
10	Newton, John	M. D	*Portsmouth*	Frontenac.
11	Nichol, James	M. D	*Perth*	Lanark.
2	Nichol, John	M. D	*Listowell*	Perth.
3	Niemeier, George	M. D	*Neustadt*	Grey.
1	Nixon, Alexander	M. D	*Napier*	Middlesex.
7	Noble, Charles T	M. D	*Georgina*	York.

. of iv.	NAME.	TITLE.	ADDRESS.	COUNTY.
9	NODEN, William	M. D	*Roseneath*	Northumberland.
8	NORRIS, George Abbott	M. D	*Omemee*	Victoria.
8	OAKLEY, Francis	M. D	*Manilla*	Victoria.
4	O'CONNOR, Maurice McN	M. D	*Haysville*	Waterloo.
6	OGDEN, Edwy Joseph	M. D	*Oakville*	Halton.
7	OGDEN, Uzziel	M. D	*Toronto*	York.
7	OGDEN, William Winslow	M. B	*Toronto*	York.
5	OILLE, Lucius Sterne	M. D	*St. Catharines*	Lincoln.
7	OLDRIGHT, William	M. B	*Toronto*	York.
0	OLIVER, Alfred Sales	M. D	*Kingston*	Frontenac.
1	OLIVER, Edward	M. D	*Moore*	Lambton.
1	OLIVER, William H	M. D	*Oil Springs*	Lambton.
6	O'REILLY, Charles	M. D	*Hamilton*	Wentworth.
5	O'REILLY, Miles	M. D	*Onondaga*	Brant.
0	ORONHYATEKHA	M. B	*Frankford*	Hastings.
7	ORR, Joseph Orlando	L. M. B	*Bond Head*	Simcoe.
3	ORTON, George T	M. D	*Fergus*	Wellington.
6	ORTON, Henry	M. D	*Ancaster*	Wentworth.
3	ORTON, Richard	M. B	*Morriston*	Wellington.
9	O'SULLIVAN, John	M. D	*Peterboro'*	Peterboro.
5	PADFIELD, Charles Wm	M. D	*Burford*	Brant.
3	PAGET, Arthur	M. D	*Elora*	Wellington.
5	PALMER, Loran L	M. D	*Thorold*	Welland.
5	PALMER, Robert N	M. B	*Brantford*	Brant.
9	PARKER, Robert	M. D	*Stirling*	Hastings.
3	PARSLEY, Wm. Henry	MRCS; Eng	*Thornbury, T'p Collingwood.*	Grey
2	PARSONS, George	MRCS; Eng	*Fullarton, Avon Bank P. O*	Perth.
2	PASMORE, William J	M. D	*West's Corners*	Perth.
3	PATERSON, James Rae	M. D	*Tiverton*	Bruce.
2	PATON, George	M. D	*Brucefield*	Huron.
1	PATTERSON, James	M. D	*Almonte*	Lanark.
5	PATTON, Franklin J	M. D	*St. George*	Brant.
6	PATTULLO, Alexander	L. M. B	*Brampton*	Peel.
8	PEAKE, John	Cer. T. S. M	*Weston*	York.
7	PEARSON, Benjamin F	M. D	*Queensville*	York.
1	PEGLEY, Rowley	MRCS; Eng	*Chatham*	Kent.
2	PENTLAND, William Ro'bt	M. B	*Shakspeare*	Perth.
2	PENWARDEN, John M	M. D	*Fingal*	Elgin.
3	PERKINS, William	M. D	*Rockwood*	Wellington.
9	PERKS, George	L. M. B	*Port Hope*	Durham.
4	PHELAN, John	L. M. B	*Pleasant Hill*	Norfolk.
7	PHILBRICK, Cornelius Jas	FRCS; Eng	*Toronto, Yorkville*	York.
4	PHILIP, David Leslie	M. D	*Plattsville*	Oxford.
4	PHILIP, John Roy	M. B	*Galt*	Waterloo.
7	PHILIPS, Martin	M. D	*Toronto*	York.
2	PHILLIPS, Thomas	MRCS; Eng	*London*	Middlesex.
6	PHILLIPS, Thomas G	M. D	*Grahamsville*	Peel.
2	PHILP, John	M. D	*Listowell*	Perth.
6	PHILP, William	M. D	*Waterdown*	Wentworth.
3	PINKERTON, James	M. D	*Ayton*	Grey.
3	PIPE, William	M. D	*Berlin*	Waterloo.
7	PLAYTER, Edward	M. B	*Schomberg*	York.
8	POLLOCK, Duncan James	M. B	*Scarboro'*	York.
3	PORTER, Robert,	M. D	*Durham*	Grey.
11	POTTER, William	L. M. B	*Gananoque*	Leeds.
10	POTTS, George Jerald	M. D	*Belleville*	Hastings.
1	POUSSETTE, Arthur C	M. D	*Sarnia*	Lambton.
9	POWELL, Newton Wm	M. D	*Cobourg*	Northumberland
10	POWER, James	MRCS; Eng	*Belleville*	Hastings.
9	POWERS, Baldwin L	M. D	*Port Hope*	Durham.
12	PRENTISS, George W	M. D	*North Plantagenet*	Prescott.
11	PRESTON, Robert H	M. D	*Newboro'*	Leeds.

No. of Div.	NAME.	TITLE.	ADDRESS.	COUNTY.
10	PRICE, Robinson Britton...	M. D......	*Bath*	Addington.
12	PRINGLE, George..........	M. D......	*Cornwall*	Stormont.
3	PRITCHARD, Frederick.....	M. D......	*Durham*................	Grey.
3	PROUDFOOT, John Smith ...	M. D	*Latona*	Grey.
9	PUGH, Frederick..........	L. M. B....	*Cobourg*...............	Northumberland
5	PYNE, Thomas............	LCPS.; LC.	*Hagersville*	Haldimand.
1	QUARRY, William Brown...	M. D......	*Lucan*	Middlesex.✓
8	RAE, Francis.............	M. B	*Oshawa*	Ontario.
3	RAMSAY, Robert...........	M. D......	*Orillia*................	Simcoe.
12	RATTRAY, Charles.........	M. D......	*Cornwall*	Stormont.
8	RAY, John Closson........	M. D......	*Vroomanton*	Ontario.
7	RAY, John Edwin..........	M. D......	*Toronto*	York.
10	REDNER, Horace P.........	M. D......	*Shannonville*	Hastings.
8	REED, John N.............	L. M. B....	*Thornhill*	York.
7	REEVE, Richard A.........	M. D......	*Toronto*	York.
6	REID, Alex. Campbell.....	M. B	*Hamilton*..............	Wentworth
8	REID, Henry R.	M. D......	*Bowmanville*	Durham.
5	REILY, Adrian............	M. D......	*Wei and*...............	Welland.
6	RICHARDSON, Henry.......	M. B	*Ancaster*	Wentworth.
7	RICHARDSON, James Henry.	MRCS; Eng	*Toronto*	York.
4	RICHARDSON, Samuel	L. M. B....	*Galt*	Waterloo.
6	RICHARDSON, William......	L. M. B....	*Nelson*	Halton.
6	RIDDALL, John Knight....	M. D......	*Alton*	Peel.
7	RIDDEL, Archibald Alex....	L. M. B....	*Toronto*	York.
10	RIDLEY, Charles Neville....	LCPS.; LC.	*Belleville*	Hastings.
6	RIDLEY, Henry Thomas....	M. D......	*Hamilton*	Wentworth.
6	ROBERTSON, David.........	M. D......	*Milton*	Halton.
11	ROBILLARD, Adolph........	M. D......	*Ottawa*	Carleton.
6	ROBINSON, Charles.........	M. D......	*Claude*	Peel.
7	ROBINSON, Thomas Slade...	LSA; Lond.	*Toronto*	York.
11	ROCHE, William P.........	M. D......	*North Gower*...........	Carleton.
7	RODGERS, David L.........	M. D......	*Newmarket*	York.
1	ROE William John........	L. M. B....	*Bothwell*	Kent.
9	ROL. s, Charles...........	L. M. B....	*Cobourg*...............	Northumberland
1	ROLLS, James A...........	M. D......	*Chatham*	Kent.
7	ROLPH, J. Widmer.........	M. D......	*Toronto*	York.
8	ROSE, William N	LRCS.; Ed.	*Newcastle*..............	Durham.
7	ROSEBRUGH, A. M.........	M. D......	*Toronto*	York.
6	ROSEBRUGH, J. W..........	M. D......	*Hamilton*	Wentworth.
9	ROSS, Thomas Keith.......	M. D	*Napanee*...............	Lennox.
7	ROSS, James..............	L. M. B....	*Toronto*	York.
4	ROUNDS, James Burley.....	M. D......	*Drumbo*	Oxford.
7	ROWELL, James...........	M. D......	*Toronto*	York.
11	RUGG, Henry C...........	M. D......	*Perth*	Lanark.
8	RUPERT, Oliver..........	M. D......	*Maple*.................	York.
7	RUSSELL, John P..........	M. D......	*Toronto*	York.
6	RUTHERFORD, Henry C.....	M. D......	*Dundas*	Wentworth.
1	RUTHERFORD, James P.....	M. D......	*Harwich*...............	Kent.
2	RUTHVEN, Duncan G.......	M. D......	*Wallacetown*	Elgin.
9	RUTTAN, Allen............	M. D......	*Napanee*	Lennox.
10	RUTTAN, Joseph Baillie....	M. D......	*Picton*	Prince Edward
6	RYALL, George............	M. B	*Hamilton*	Wentworth.
6	RYALL, Isaac.............	M. B	*Hamilton*	Wentworth.
4	SALMON, James Moon......	L. M. B....	*Simcoe*	Norfolk.
4	SALMON, John	M. D......	*Simcoe*	Norfolk.
3	SANDERSON, George Wm...	M. D......	*Orillia*	Simcoe.
1	SANDS, Richmond..........	L. M. B....	*Nairn*.................	Middlesex.✓
7	SANGSTER, John Herbert...	M. D......	*Yorkville*	York.
11	SAVAGE, Alex. Charles.....	M. D......	*Ottawa*	Carleton.
8	SAVAGE, Thomas Young...	M. D......	*Thistletown*	York.
3	SAVAGE, William F........	M. D......	*Elora*	Wellington.
7	SCHOLFIELD, Thomas C.....	M. D......	*Bond Head*.............	Simcoe.
7	SCHOLFIELD, William......	M. D......	*Lloydtown*	York.
5	SCHOOLEY, Jay Wesley....	M. D......	*Welland*...............	Welland.

No. of Div.	NAME.	TITLE.	ADDRESS.	COUNTY.
4	Scott, Henry H	M. D	*Ingersoll*	Oxford.
4	Scott, William	L. M. B	*Woodstock*	Oxford.
12	Scott, William James		*Prescott*	Grenville.
8	Scott, William Sumner	M. D	*Saugeen*	Bruce.
1	Seager, Charles	L. M. B	*Sarnia*	Lambton.
3	Second, Solomon	M. D	*Kincardine*	Bruce.
2	Shaver, Peter Rolph	M. D	*Stratford*	Perth.
1	Shirley, Joseph W	M. D	*Watford*	Lambton.
1	Shoebottam, Henry	M. D	*Sarnia*	Lambton.
2	Sill Abraham	M. D	*Listowell*	Perth.
12	Sinclair, Archibald C	M. D	*Martintown*	Glengarry.
1	Sinclair, Daniel Alex	M. D	*Melbourne, Longwood P.O*	Middlesex.
2	Sinclair, John	M. B	*St. Marys*	Perth.
10	Skinner, Henry	M. D	*Kingston*	Frontenac.
6	Skinner, Ormond	LCPS; L.C.	*Waterdown*	Wentworth.
3	Sloane, Allan C	M. B	*Speedie*	Grey.
2	Sloan, William	M. D	*Blyth*	Huron.
2	Smale, Samuel B	M. B	*Wroxeter*	Huron.
3	Smith, Daniel	M. B	*Drayton*	Wellington.
12	Smith, Daniel D	M. D	*Cornwall*	Stormont.
1	Smith, Jacob	L. M. B	*Ridgetown*	Kent.
8	Smith, James W	M. D	*Raglan*	Ontario.
10	Smith, John Robert	M. D	*Harrowsmith*	Frontenac.
1	Smith, Robert R	M. D	*Komoka*	Middlesex.
1	Smith, William E	M. D	*Falkirk*	Middlesex.
6	Smith, William L	M. D	*Glanford*	Wentworth.
2	Smith, William R	L. M. B	*Seaforth*	Huron.
1	Somerville, James A	M. D	*Strathroy*	Middlesex.
2	Southwick, George	L. M. B	*St. Thomas*	Elgin.
12	Sparham, Emanuel B	L. M. B	*Kemptville*	Grenville.
12	Sparham, Eric B	M. D	*Brockville*	Leeds.
10	Sparham, George S	M. D	*Waterloo, K'n*	Frontenac.
4	Sparks, Thomas	L. M. B	*Lakeside, East Nissouri*	Oxford.
8	Spooner, George D	M. D	*Newtonville, Clark P.O*	Durham.
2	Srigley, Nelson	L. M. B	*Wingham*	Huron.
2	Stanbury, Richard	M. D	*Bayfield*	Huron.
4	Stanton, George	M. D	*Simcoe*	Norfolk.
9	Stark, John D	M. D	*Norwood*	Peterboro'.
3	Stephens, Alexander R	L. M. B	*Collingwood*	Simcoe.
12	Stephenson, James	M. D	*Iroquois*	Dundas.
8	Stevenson, James D	M. D	*Kleinburg*	York.
6	Stewart, Alexander	M. D	*Mono Mills*	Peel.
3	Stewart, Alex. John	M. D	*Orillia*	Simcoe.
11	Stewart, James	M. D	*Duncanville*	Russell.
11	Stewart, James D	M. D	*Ottawa*	Carleton.
4	Stewart, James W	M. D	*Port Dover*	Norfolk.
10	Stewart, John	LRCS.; Ed.	*Kingston*	Frontenac.
2	Stewart, Peter	M. D	*Fingal*	Elgin.
10	Stewart, Robert	L. M. B	*Belleville*	Hastings.
5	Stimson, James	M. D.	*St. George*	Brant.
11	St. Jean, Peter	LCPS; L.C.	*Ottawa*	Carleton.
8	Stokes, Charles S	M. D	*Columbus*	Ontario.
3	Stone, Robert Winn	M. D	*Salem, Winford*	Wellington.
6	Strange, Henry	M. D	*Hamilton*	Wentworth.
10	Strange, Orlando S	M. D	*Kingston*	Frontenac.
6	Street, William H	M. D	*Milton*	Halton.
2	Stubbs, Joseph	M. D	*Kirkton*	Huron.
10	Sullivan, Michael	M. D	*Kingston*	Frontenac.
6	Sutherland, Thomas J	M. D	*Oakville*	Halton.
9	Sutton, Henry H	M. B	*Madoc*	Hastings.
4	Swan, Levi H	M. D	*Embro*	Oxford.
11	Sweetland, John	M. D	*Ottawa*	Carleton.
1	Swisher, Richard D	M. D	*Thamesville*	Kent.
7	Symes, James	LRCS; Irel.	*Bond Head*	Simcoe.

No. of Div.	NAME.	TITLE.	ADDRESS.	COUNTY.
3	Syme, Thomas F	L. M. B	*Meaford*	Grey.
2	Tamlyn, John E	M. D	*Manchester, Auburn P.O.*	Huron.
3	Taylor, James	M. D	*Tara*	Bruce.
7	Taylor, Wm. Henry	M. B	*Bradford*	Simcoe.
5	Tegart, Edwin W	M. D	*Scotland*	Brant.
7	Tempest, William	M. B	*Toronto*	York.
7	Temple, James A	M. D	*Toronto*	York.
3	Tennant, John S	M. D	*Lucknow*	Bruce.
3	Thom, John Condie	M. B	*Garafraxa*	Wellington.
1	Thom, John James	M. D	*Windsor*	Essex.
2	Thompson, Alexander	M. D	*Blyth*	Huron.
7	Thorburn, James	M. D	*Toronto*	York.
5	Thorburn, Richard	M. B	*Queenston*	Lincoln.
3	Thornbury, Thomas John	Cer. T. S. M	*Singhampton*	Grey.
11	Thornton, William M	M. D	*Perth*	Lanark.
10	Thwaites, James	LSA ; Lond.	*Ameliasburg*	Prince Edward.
9	Tisdale, John Cass	M. B	*Cold Springs*	Northumberland.
2	Tracey, Robert	M. D	*Seaforth*	Huron.
3	Tuck, Herbert F	M. D	*Guelph*	Wellington.
8	Tucker, David	M. B	*Pickering*	Ontario.
5	Tufford, Charles D	M. D	*Brantford*	Brant.
9	Turner, Henry	M. D	*Millbrook*	Durham.
9	Turner, John	M. D	*Baltimore*	Northumberland.
4	Turquand, John	L.M.B	*Woodstock*	Oxford.
2	Tweedale, John B	M. D	*Vienna*	Elgin.
8	Tweedie, Gilbert	M. D	*Lindsay*	Victoria.
1	Tye, George A	M. D	*Thamesville*	Kent.
3	Ussher, Henry	M. D	*Walkerton*	Bruce.
2	Vail, Charles L	M. B	*Vienna*	Elgin.
3	Vallack, Adoniah	MRCS ; Eng	*Collingwood*	Simcoe.
7	Valentine, John	L.M.B	*Toronto*	York.
11	Valade, Francis	LCPS ; L.C.	*Ottawa*	Carleton.
1	Vanvelsor, Daniel J	M. D	*Blenheim*	Kent.
3	Vardon, William H	M. D	*Hawksville*	Waterloo.
3	Vardon, Thomas Wyre	M. D	*Hawksville*	Waterloo.
7	Vaux, Harry E	M. D	*Schomberg*	York.
2	Vercoe, Henry L	M. D	*Egmondville*	Huron.
9	Wade, William	M. D	*Cobourg*	Northumberland.
7	Wadsworth, James J	M. B	*Simcoe*	Norfolk.
7	Wadsworth, Andrew H. B.	M. B	*Toronto*	York.
3	Walden, John William	M. D	*Wellesley*	Waterloo.
2	Walden, Benjamin	M. D	*Winchelsea*	Huron.
4	Walbank, Samuel S	L. M. B	*Ingersoll*	Oxford.
6	Walker, Allan H	M. D	*Dundas*	Wentworth.
5	Walker, James	M. D	*Nanticoke*	Haldimand.
4	Walker, Nathaniel O	M. D.	*Port Dover*	Norfolk.
4	Walker, Robert	M. D	*Woodhouse*	Norfolk.
3	Wallace, James	M. B	*Alma*	Wellington.
12	Wallace, James M	L.M.B	*Spencerville*	Grenville.
9	Wallace, Samuel	M. D	*Campbellford*	Northumberland.
8	Warren, Henry	M. D	*Brooklin*	Ontario.
9	Waters, George	M. B	*Cobourg*	Northumberland.
6	Webster, Samuel	L.M.B	*Norval*	Halton.
1	Weir, Richard	M. D	*Warwick*	Lambton.
2	Weir, William	M. D	*Merrickville*	Grenville.
6	Weeks, William J	M. D	*Wellington Square*	Halton.
6	White, Thomas	M. B	*Hamilton*	Wentworth.
8	Whiteside, William N	M. B	*Little Britain*	Victoria.
10	Williams, Richard W	M. B	*Trenton*	Hastings.
4	Williams, Joseph A	M. D	*Ingersoll*	Oxford.
6	Williams, J. S. W	M. D	*Oakville*	Halton.
6	Williams, Moses H	M. D	*Toronto*	York.
4	Willson, John	MRCS ; Eng	*Simcoe*	Norfolk.
10	Willson, Benjamin S	M. D	*Roslin*	Hastings.

No. of Div.	NAME.	TITLE.	ADDRESS.	COUNTY.
9	WILLSON, Robert M.	M. D.	*Cobourg*	Northumberland.
5	WILSON, George D.	M. D.	*Burford*	Brant.
2	WILSON, John H.	M. D.	*St. Thomas*	Elgin.
11	WILSON, William.	C. M.	*Carleton Place*	Lanark.
11	WILSON William.	M. D.	*Ottawa*	Carleton.
6	WINN, Theophilus B.	M. B.	*Nassagaweya*	Halton.
7	WINSTANLEY, Orlando S.	MRCS; Eng	*Toronto*	York.
6	WOOD, James M.	M. D.	*Streetsville*	Peel.
3	WOOD, John W.	M. D.	*Durham*	Grey.
11	WOOD, Orrin C.	L.M.B	*Ottawa*	Carleton.
2	WOODS, Ninian.	M. D.	*Bayfield*	Huron.
5	WOOLVERTON, Algernon	M. D.	*Grimsby*	Lincoln
5	WOOLVERTON, Jonathan	M. D.	*Grimsby*	Lincoln.
7	WORKMAN, Benjamin	M. D.	*Toronto*	York.
7	WORKMAN, Joseph.	M. D.	*Toronto*	York.
2	WORTHINGTON, Addison	LCPS; L.C.	*Wroxeter*	Huron.
6	WRIGHT, David D.	M. D.	*Oakville*	Halton.
7	WRIGHT, Henry H.	LCPS; U.C.	*Toronto*	York.
3	WRIGHT, George W.	M. D.	*Griersville*	Grey.
7	WRIGHT, George	M.B	*Toronto*	York.
2	WYE, John H.	M. D.	*Dungannon*	Huron.
3	WYLIE, Thomas.	M. D.	*Duntroon*	Simcoe.
10	YATES, Horatio	M. D.	*Kingston*	Frontenac.
10	YATES, Octavius	M. D.	*Kingston*	Frontenac.
3	YEOMANS, Horace P.	M. D.	*Mount Forest*	Wellington.
3	YORK, Thomas J.	M. D.	*Hillsburg*	Wellington.
5	YOUMANS, Milton	M. D.	*Hagersville*	Haldimand.
9	YOUNG, Daniel.	M. D.	*Conway*	Lennox.
2	YOUNG, John	MRCS; Eng	*Kinburn*	Huron.

PERSONS not included in the foregoing list who are entitled to vote.

No. of Div.	NAME.	TITLE.	ADDRESS.	COUNTY.
9	BOUCHER, Robert P	M. D.	*Peterboro'*	Peterboro'.
11	CHURCH, Coller M	M. D.	*Goulbourne*	Carleton.
2	FRASER, Donald M.	M. D.	*London*	Middlesex.
8	HILLIER, Salmon C.	M. D.	*Enniskillen*	Durham.
8	HILLIER, William	M. D.	*Enniskillen*	Durham.
11	LYNN, James P.	M. D.	*Renfrew*	Renfrew.
6	LANGS, Major S.	M. D.	*Lynden*	Wentworth.

PERSONS included in the foregoing list who have removed while these pages were going through the press.

No. of Div.	NAME.	TITLE.	ADDRESS.	COUNTY.
8	BRADLEY, Benj. Lorenzo	M. D.	*Newcastle*	Durham.
10	INGERSOLL, Isaac F	M. D.	*Picton*	Prince Edward.
3	JONES, Charles A.	M. D.	*Holstein*	Grey.
12	KERTLAND, Edwin H	M. D.	*Brockville*	Leeds.

PERSONS REGISTERED, but residing out of the Province.

NAME.	TITLE.	ADDRESS.
CARROLL, John Adams..................	M. D......	*447 2nd Avenue, New York.*
CORSON, John W........................	M. D......	*New York.*
FRASER, Hugh Allan.....	LRCPS; K'n	*Waverley Place, New York.*
JONES, Leslie.........................	LRCS.; Ed.	*England.*
LANGRELL, Richard Thomas............	M. D......	*Eau Claire, Wisconsin.*
MICKLE, William J......................	M. B......	*England.*
McPHERSON, William..................	LFPS; Glas	*Bay City, Michigan.*

ERRATA.

Page 27. The number of Robert B. Aylsworth's Territorial Division should read not 12.

" 31. The number of George Dunham's Division should read 11, not 12.

" 32. The number of John G. Giles' Division should read 11, not 12

" 32. Gilmore, William R., should read *Gilmor, William R.*

" 32. The number of E. B. Haight's Division should read 11, not 12.

" 33. The number of Archibald Imeson's Division should read 11, not 12.

A BY-LAW

To regulate the holding of Elections of Homœopathic and Eclectic Representatives in the Medical Council, under the Ontario Medical Act.

[Passed April 8, 1869.]

Preamble.—WHEREAS, power has been granted to the Medical Council in the Ontario Medical Act, to make By-laws to regulate the manner of holding the Elections under the said Act; be it therefore enacted as follows:

1.—This By-law shall only apply to the Election of Homœopathic and Eclectic Members of the Council.

2.—That the Homœopathic Members of the College of Physicians and Surgeons of Ontario shall meet at the Queen's Hotel, in the City of Toronto, on the first Tuesday in June, at 2 o'clock p. m., to make arrangements for the Election to take place on the following Tuesday.

3.—That there shall be appointed at this meeting three Scrutineers for said Election, who shall be Homœopathic members of said College of Physicians and Surgeons of Ontario; and that such Homœopathic members of the said College who may be unable to attend this meeting may, nevertheless, vote for the appointment of said Scrutineers, by sending their votes, duly signed, to the Secretary of the Homœopathic Medical Board, in a sealed envelope by mail, and such Votes being recorded by the said Secretary shall have the same value as if the voters were personally present.

4.—That the Scrutineers so appointed shall forthwith cause voting papers to be sent to every Homœopathic member of the said College of Physicians and Surgeons, of Ontario, by mail, with instructions that the names of the five Homœopathic members he may desire to elect as his representatives in the Council of the said College be legibly inscribed on said paper, which is to be returned by mail to the Secretary of the Homœopathic Medical Board, without delay, in a sealed or duly closed envelope, marked on the outside, "Vote for Homœpathic members of the College of Physicians and Surgeons of Ontario."

5.—That the Secretary of the Homœopathic Medical Board shall, on the second Tuesday in June, in presence of the Scrutineers above referred to, open the envelopes containing the votes, and the five names having the highest number of votes shall be returned to the Registrar of the Council of the College of Physicians and Surgeons of Ontario, as Homœopathic members of the said Council for the next three years.

6.—If, upon examining the voting papers, it shall appear that there is an equality between two or more, having the lowest number of votes, it shall be lawful for the Scrutineers mentioned in Section 3 of this By-law, to decide by lot which of these names thus equal shall be chosen as representative.

7.—That in the event of the unavoidable absence of any of the Scrutineers appointed at the meeting to be held under Section 2 of this By-Law, on the first Tuesday in June, it shall be lawful for the other Scrutineers and the Secretary of the Homœopathic Medical Board to nominate some other Homœopathic member of the said College of Physicians and Surgeons to act as Scrutineer in his stead.

8.—That the present Officers and members of the Homœopathic Medical Board shall be eligible as Scrutineers.

9.—That the Scrutineers shall themselves be eligible as representatives.

10.—Wherever the words "Homœopathic Members" or "Homœopathic Medical Board" occur in the preceding sections of this By-Law, they shall be construed to mean "Eclectic Members" and "Eclectic Medical Board," respectively, in their application to the election of the Eclectic Members of the Council of the College of Physicians and Surgeons of Ontario; and it shall be understood that the same provisions shall be applicable to the election of Eclectic Members of the said Council as are applied to the election of Homœopathic Members.

LIST

of Homœopathic Members of the College of Physicians and Surgeons of Ontario.

NAME.	TITLE.	ADDRESS.	COUNTY.
Adams, Joseph	M. D.	*Toronto*	York.
Aikman, Peter Augustus	L.H.M.B.	*Colchester*	Essex.
Allen, Henry C.	M. D.	*Brantford*	Brant.
Allen, Thomas E.	M. D.	*St. Catharines*	Lincoln.
Brodrick, Henry McAdam	L.H.M.B.	*Chatham*	Kent.
Campbell, Clarence Thomas	C.H.M.B.	*London*	Middlesex.
Campbell, George W.	L.H.M.B.	*Crediton*	Huron.
Caulton, Frederick George	L.H.M.B.	*St. Catharines*	Lincoln.
Clark, Charles Whitfield	M. D.	*Aylmer*	Elgin.
Clark, George Frederick	M. D.	*Aylmer*	Elgin.
Cleveland, William Knapp	L H.M.B.	*St. Catharines*	Lincoln.
Cowan, William Brown	M. D.	*Guelph*	Wellington.
Crawford, Lambert Ferguson	M. D.	*Hamilton*	Wentworth.
*Danter, James F.	M. D.	*Goderich*	Huron.
D'yfoot, Herbert Michael	L.H M.B.	*Rochester*	New York.
Elliot, Charles S.	M. D.	*Orillia*	Simcoe.
Fergusson, John William	M. D.	*Hamilton*	Wentworth.
Field, Gilbert Chrysler	M. D.	*Woodstock*	Oxford.
Fry, William	C.H.M.B.	*Dunnville*	Haldimand.
Hall, John	M. D.	*Toronto*	York.
Harvey, Leander	L.H.M.B.	*Watford*	Lambton.
Henderson, Gregg	L.H.M.B.	*Strathroy*	Middlesex.
Husband, George Edmund	M. D.	*Galt*	Waterloo.
Job, Charles Conliffe	M. D.	*Galt*	Waterloo.
Lancaster, David Henry	M. D.	*Culloden*	Oxford.
Lancaster, Joseph J.	M. D.	*London*	Middlesex.
Logan, George	M. D.	*Ottawa*	Carleton.
Luton, Leonard	M. D.	*St. Thomas*	Elgin.
McDonald, Peter	M. D.	*Ingersoll*	Oxford.
McLaughlin, Alexander	C.H.M.B.	*Dunnville*	Elgin.
McLaughlin, Miar	L.H.M.B.	*Fingal*	Norfolk.
*McLean, John	M. D	*Port Rowan*	Haldimand.
Morden, Ralph J. P.	M. D.	*London*	Middlesex.
Nichol, Thomas	M. D.	*Belleville*	Hastings.
Nichol, William	L.H.M.B.	*Burford*	Brant.
Oliphant, David Sewall	M. D.	*Toronto*	York.
Poole, Thomas Wesley	M. D.	*Lindsay*	Victoria.
Smith, William Lemuel	C.H.M.B.	*London*	Middlesex.
Springer, Oliver	M. D.	*Chatham*	Kent.
Springer, William	M. D.	*Ingersoll*	Oxford.
Tisdale, Allan Napier	M. D.	*Otterville*	Oxford.
Traver, Gilbert Ryerson	L.H.M.B.	*London*	Middlesex.
Tripp, Moses Edward	L.H.M.B.	*Ingersoll*	Oxford.
Tripp, John W	L.H.M.B.	*Port Burwell*	Elgin.
Vernon, Elias	M. D.	*Hamilton*	Wentworth.
Wanless, John	M. D.	*Montreal*	
Wanless, John Robson	M. D.	*Montreal*	
Westland, George Philip	L.H.M.B.	*London*	Middlesex.
York, Winford	M. D.	*Simcoe*	Norfolk.

L. H. M. B. is an abbreviation for Licentiate of the Homœopathic Medical Board of Upper Canada—and it is to be understood that the person has received a Provincial License—granted under the authority of the Act, chap. 41, *Con. Stat., U. C.*

C. H. M. B. is an abbreviation for Certificate of the Homœpathic Medical Board.

*Registered as an Eclectic also.

LIST

of Eclectic Members of the College of Physicians and Surgeons of Ontario.

NAME.	TITLE.	ADDRESS.	COUNTY.
Armstrong, William........	L.E.M.B.	*Orangeville...... ....*	Wellington.
Bell, William Ralph.........	M. D.....	*New Edinburgh......... .*	Carleton.
Bradley, Thomas...........	L E M B..	*Pervie ....*	Bruce.
Brawn, Wm. H. G...... ...	C E.M B..	*Exeter ....*	Huron.
Bright, James Cook.........	L.E.M.B .	*Chatham ....*	Kent.
Brown, John Henry..........	M D.....	*Waterdown ....*	Wentworth.
Burns, Robert..............	M. D	*Pakenham.............*	Lanark.
Chamberlain, George.........	M. D.. ..	*Westover ....*	Wentworth.
Clarke, George A.....	M. D.....	*Ingersoll ....*	Oxford.
Clarke, Richard Hare........	M. D....	*Cobourg. ....*	Northumberland.
Cornell, Seth Shaw..........	M D.....	*Toledo ....*	Leeds.
Cowen, Young...............	M. D....	*Exeter ....*	Huron.
*Danter James F............	M. D.....	*Goderich ....*	Huron.
Devlin James Alphonsus.....	M. D.....	*Hamilton ....*	Wentworth.
Edwards, George W.........	C.E.M B..	*Addison ....*	Leeds.
Fenton, Wakefield...........	C E M.B .	*Bowmanville ....*	Durham.
Fowler, John Milton...... ..	M. D.....	*Burford ....*	Brant.
Frickleton, Joshua Dier......	C E.M.B .	*Southampton...............*	Bruce.
Giesea, Frederick A.........	M. D.....	*Smithuille ....*	Lincoln.
G[illegible]o, Henry P............	M. D.....	*Port Hope..............*	Durham.
Hall, James John.......... ..	M. D.....	*St. Marys..............*	Perth.
Hollingshead, Silas...... ..	L.E.M.B .	*Toronto ....*	York.
Hopkins, Nicholas, Junior....	M. D.....	*Dunnville ....*	Haldimand.
Hopkins, Nicholas, Senior.....	M. D.....	*Dunnville ....*	Haldimand.
Hossack, Thomas...........	L.E.M.B .	*Lucan.... ....*	Middlesex.
James, Henry...............	M. D.....	*Belleville ....*	Hastings.
Kay, John Paterson..........	L.E.M.B .	*Culross, Belmore P. O.....*	Bruce.
Knight, James................	L.E.M.B .	*Tamworth ....*	Addington.
Lake, Samuel Knapp.........	L.E.M.B .	*Bloomfield ....*	Prince Edward.
*McLean, John	M. D.....	*Port Rowan..............*	Norfolk.
McQuillan, Robert..........	M. D.....	*Madoc ....*	Hastings.
McTaggart, Miles F.........	C.E.M.B..	*Belleville ....*	Hastings.
Michener, Joseph H..........	L.E.M.B .	*Ridgeway..............*	Welland.
Morrison, Joseph...........	M. D.....	*Kemptville ....*	Grenville.
Mott, George..............	L.E.M.B .	*Wyoming................*	Lambton.
Munger, James Sylvester. ...	M. D.....	*Aldborough........ .....*	Elgin.
Nesbitt, Francis Lucas......	M. D.....	*Woodstock ....*	Oxford.
Noxon, Allan.......	M. D.....	*Almonte.................*	Lanark.
Patterson, Bradford.	M. D.....	*Bowmanville ....*	Durham.
Patterson, William.........	M. D.....	*Frankford ....*	Hastings.
Pitcher, Charles Pettit.	M. D.....	*Jordan ....*	Lincoln.
Robinson, William Odell.....	L.E.M.B .	*St. Jacobs...............*	Waterloo.
Rollins, James............ .	L.E M.B..	*Exeter ....*	Huron.
Roome, William F.........	M. D.....	*Newbury ....*	Middlesex.
Sinclair, John McNab........	M. D.....	*Delta....................*	Leeds.
Steifelmeyer, John Ulrich....	L E.M.B .	*New Hamburg............*	Perth.
Terryberry, Jacob Gilbert...	M. D.....	*Burford ....*	Brant.
Walden, Francis............	L E M.B .	*Lucan ....*	Middlesex.
Walker, Isaac Ralph.........	M. D.....	*Ingersoll ....*	Oxford.
Wood, George William.......	M D.....	*Delhi...............*	Oxford.
Yeagsley, Henry......... ...	L.E.M.B .	*Waterloo ....*	Waterloo.

L. E. M. B. is an abbreviation for Licentiate of the Eclectic Medical Board, and it is to be understood that the person has received a Provincial License granted under the authority of the Act passed in the twenty-fourth year of Her Majesty's reign, chapter 110, *Statutes of Canada.*

C. E .M. B. is an abbreviation for Certificate of the Eclectic Medical Board.

* Registered as a Homœopathist also.

LIST OF QUALIFICATIONS

WHICH ENTITLE TO REGISTRATION.

CANADIAN:

Licentiate of the Medical Board of Upper Canada.
Licentiate of either Quebec or Montreal Medical Board.
Licentiate of the College of Physicians and Surgeons of Upper Canada.
Licentiate of the College of Physicians and Surgeons of Lower Canada.
Doctor of Medicine, Doctor of Medicine and Surgery, or Doctor of Medicine and Master of Surgery, of the University of McGill College.
Doctor or Bachelor of Medicine, Laval University.
Doctor or Bachelor of Medicine of the University of Toronto.
Doctor or Bachelor of Medicine, Trinity College, Toronto.
Doctor of Medicine of the University of Victoria College.
Doctor of Medicine of the University of Queen's College.
Fellow or Licentiate of the Royal College of Physicians and Surgeons of Kingston.
Certificate of qualification of the Toronto School of Medicine.
Licentiate of the Homœopathic Medical Board of Upper Canada.
Licentiate of the Eclectic Medical Board of Upper Canada.

BRITISH:

Fellow, Member, Licentiate, or Extra Licentiate, of the Royal College of Physicians of London.
Fellow, Member, or Licentiate, of the Royal College of Physicians of Edinburgh.
Fellow, Member, or Licentiate in Midwifery, of the Royal College of Surgeons of England.
Fellow or Licentiate of the Royal College of Surgeons of Edinburgh.
Fellow or Licentiate of the Faculty of Physicians and Surgeons of Glasgow.
Fellow, Licentiate, or Licentiate in Midwifery, of the Royal College of Surgeons of Ireland.
Fellow, Licentiate in Medicine, or Licentiate in Midwifery, of the King's and Queen's College of Physicians of Ireland.
Licentiate of the Society of Apothecaries, London.
Licentiate of the Apothecaries' Hall, Dublin.
Doctor, Bachelor, or Licentiate in Medicine, of the University of Oxford.
Doctor, Bachelor, or Licentiate in Medicine, of the University of Cambridge.

BRITISH.—(*Continued.*)

Doctor, Bachelor, Licentiate in Medicine, or Master in Surgery, of the University of Durham.

Doctor or Bachelor of Medicine of the University of London.

Doctor, Bachelor of Medicine, or Master in Surgery, of the University, Aberdeen.

Doctor, Bachelor, Licentiate in Medicine, Master in Surgery, or Licentiate in Surgery, of the University of Dublin.

Doctor of Medicine, Master in Surgery, or Licentiate in Surgery, of the Queen's University in Ireland.

Doctor of Medicine of the University of Edinburgh.

Doctor of Medicine of the University of St. Andrew's.

Doctor, Bachelor, or Licentiate in Medicine, of the University and Trinity College, Dublin.

Doctor of Medicine, or Master in Surgery, of the University of Glasgow.

Doctor or Bachelor of Medicine of the University and King's College, Aberdeen.

Doctor or Bachelor of Medicine of Marischall College and University, Aberdeen.

Commission or Warrant as Physician or Surgeon in Her Majesty's Naval or Military Service.

Besides the above, graduates in Medicine and Surgery of Universities or Colleges of India and Australia are entitled to Registration, subject to the same regulations as holders of any of the above diplomas.

*** None of the Diplomas above mentioned, if granted after the 23rd day of July, 1869, will entitle the holder to registration without he passes the examination to be established by the Medical Council.

REGISTRATION FEES.

The fees for registration are as follows :—

To all whose qualifications are dated anterior to 1st July, 1865, and who register before the 23rd of January, 1870.. $ 5 00

To all whose qualifications are dated since the 1st July, 1865............ ... .$10 00

After the 23rd of January, 1870, the fee, in every case, will be..$10 00

PROVINCIAL SECRETARY'S OFFICE,
Ottawa, 29th June, 1869.

Notice is hereby given that the following curriculum of Professional Studies, established by "the General Council of Medical Education and Registration of Upper Canada," has been approved by His Excellency the Governor General in Council, in terms of sec. 17 of the Act 29 Victoria, chapter 34.

1. That no professional degree or Licence be granted to any person under twenty-one years of age.

2. That all students be required to pass an examination in general education before commencing their professional studies.

3. That four years of professional study be required after having passed the examination in general education, except as hereinafter provided.

4. From a student who is a graduate in arts of any recognized College or University, only three years of attendance upon Medical lectures shall be required.

5. That the professional examinations be divided into at least two distinct parts, that the first part may be undergone after the completion of two years of study, and the final after the termination of four years of study.

6. That the professional examination be conducted partly in writing and partly *viva voce.* And that such parts as admit of it to made as practical and demonstrative as possible.

7. No candidate shall be entitled to registration who has not attended lectures for a period of three sessions of, at least, six months each, in a University, College, or School of Medicine approved of.

8. Candidates for final examination shall furnish testimonials of having attended two full courses of lectures upon the following branches of Medical education, viz:—"Anatomy," "Chemistry," "Theory and Practice of Medicine," "Principles and Practice of Surgery, Midwifery and diseases of women and children," "Materia Medica and Pharmacy," "Practical Anatomy," "Institutes of Medicine."

Two courses of three months each, upon the following branches, viz:— "Clinical Medicine," and "Clinical Surgery."

And one course of three months upon each of the following branches, viz:—

"Medical Jurisprudence," "Practical Chemistry," and "Botany."

9. The candidate must also give proof of having attended the practice of some general Hospital, or other Hospital approved of, for the period of twelve months.

10. No one shall be permitted to become candidates for final examination whose final course embraced less than four subjects, each six months.

11. All Students shall present evidence of their having compounded Medicine for a period of twelve months, or for two periods of six months each, in the office of a regularly qualified Medical practitioner. And they shall present evidence of having attended not fewer than six cases of Midwifery.

12. The Primary professional examination shall comprise the following branches, viz: "Anatomy," "Chemistry," "Materia Medica," "Institutes of Medicine," and "Botany."

The final examination shall comprise the subjects of "Anatomy," (excluding that of the bones, muscles and ligaments,) "Practical Chemistry," "Medical Jurisprudence," "Theory and Practice of Medicine," "Principles and Practice of Surgery," and "Midwifery."

13. Four-fifths of the actual teaching days of a session must have been attended before a certificate of attendance at said session can be granted, except in case of sickness.

14. Students shall not be permitted to attend any other lectures during their first year than those on the branches comprised in the primary examination; nor will the certificate of any lecturer be recognized who lectures on more than one branch of medical science; nor must he deliver more than one lecture daily—but the Professor of Surgery may lecture on Clinical Surgery, the Professor of Medicine may lecture on Clinical Medicine, or the Professor of Materia Medica may lecture on Botany or Medical Jurisprudence.

15. All *graduates* from recognized Colleges in the United States shall matriculate and attend one full course of lectures, and all *Students* shall matriculate and complete a course of study in the College in which they intend to graduate equivalent to the curriculum required by the Council.

16. The several Colleges and Licensing Bodies shall notify the Registrar of the various examinations held by them, in order that one or more members of the Medical Council may be present.

17. The various Medical Schools and Licensing Bodies shall make returns to the Medical Council, stating the number and names of the candidates who have passed their first and second examinations, and the number of those who have been rejected at their first and second examinations, respectively. Such returns to be made annually on the first of May.

By Command,

WM. McDOUGALL, *Secretary.*

SHORT COMMENTARIES

on portions of the Medical Act.

Section 2.

The Homœopathic and Eclectic Medical Boards are completely dissolved by this Section, from and after the 8th day of June, 1869.

Section 4.

The latter part of this Section, commencing with the words "nor of modifying or restricting" etc., are without any effect; for, even granting that Section XXXVI. of Dr. Parker's Act (29 *Vic.*, *cap.* 34) is still in force, there can be no doubt that Section I. of the Act now in force completely repeals the Acts* which were guarded by Section XXXVI. of Dr. Parker's Act.

The clause in question ought to have been struck out of the Bill before it received the sanction of the Governor; but it would appear to have escaped notice.

Section 8.

Sub-Section 2.—This Sub-Section requires that those who vote for Homœopathic or Eclectic representatives in the Council, shall be licensed practitioners in Homœopathy and the Eclectic system of Medicine, respectively. Any registered practitioner is eligible as a representative of either the Homœopathic or Eclectic bodies.

Sub-Section 3.—A representative of a Territorial Division must be a registered practitioner, residing in the Division which he represents. The persons entitled to vote are all persons registered, except those who are entitled to vote for Homœopathic or Eclectic members of the Council.

This point has been frequently misinterpreted. Though why it should be, it is difficult to see. If Sub-Sections two and three are read consecutively, there will be no misunderstanding; for, in sub-section three, we see that the members of Territorial Divisions "shall be elected" * * *"from AMONGST AND BY the registered members of the profession, OTHER than those mentioned in the next preceding Sub-Section."*

---

* The Act, chapter forty-one of the Consolidated Statutes of Upper Canada (*incorporating the Homœopathists*), and the Act passed in the twenty-fourth year of Her Majesty's reign, chapter one hundred and ten (*incorporating the Eclectics*), and all Acts amending any of the said Acts.

Section 23.

This Section does not, as many seem to suppose, require old practitioners, who may neglect to register, to pass an examination before the Council, if they do not register within six months after the present Act came into force (*that is, before the* 23*rd day of July*, 1869). The owner of any one of the qualifications mentioned in Schedule A of the Act, can be registered at any time, *without examination*, upon complying with the ordinary rules relating thereto, provided the qualification in question was conferred prior to the 23rd day of July, 1869. Those who become possessed of any of the qualifications mentioned above after the 23rd day of July, 1869, must pass an examination before the Council Board of Examiners before they can be registered.

Section 25.

The Examining Board will be composed of twelve members, three of whom must be Teachers in Medicine—that is, one from the University of Victoria College, one from the Royal College of Physicians and Surgeons of Kingston, and one from the Toronto School of Medicine. The remaining nine must be registered practioners, who have no connection with any of the above-named teaching bodies.

There may be two more, who will have very limited duties—merely to examine candidates who wish to be registered as Homœopathists or Eclectics in the special branches excepted in the latter part of this section. I have said there *may be* two more; this, though, is not very clearly defined. It may be that two of the twelve will be elected by the Homœopathic and Eclectic members of Council—one each—or it may be that these sub-sections of the Council will approve of two of the twelve elected by the Council—one each—and that candidates for registration as members of either of these bodies will be allowed to pass before them.

In reference to this matter, the Registrar can not pretend to decide authoritatively; he has therefore only pointed out possible ways of complying with this section. The only thing which is certain is, that the whole number must be elected by the Council as a Council. It is for the Council to say whether two of the twelve shall be nominated by the Homœopathic and Eclectic sections of the Council, or whether two additional ones shall be added for the special purposes mentioned.

Section 30.

A large amount of discretionary power is here given to the Registrar, which it is perhaps impossible to avoid, though it would be much more satisfactory to that officer to be relieved of the responsibility which is inseparable from the exercise of discretionary power. The Registrar is often thought to be unreasonably strict in requiring proof of qualification, beyond the presentation of the documents conferring the right to registration. The fact of his having generally required something more has brought him into frequent collision with members of the profession, and has had the effect of producing a degree of irritation and hard feeling on the part of many towards him, which has been extremely unpleasant. For this reason the writer believes it will be advantageous to state, in this connection, the line of action which his past experience as Registrar has led him to pursue, and the reasons why he believes the precautions he has taken to be necessary.

The law only requires that the Registrar shall be satisfied by the proper evidence that the person claiming is entitled to registration. The production of the diploma to be registered is required at present, with an affidavit made before some County Judge, in which the applicant swears that he is the person named and intended in the diploma exhibited, and that the diploma is what it purports to be—that is, genuine.

The only cases in which the Registrar can safely dispense with this affidavit are those in which he is personally acquainted with the applicant, and is cognizant of the fact that the applicant actually received the qualification requisite; even then the affidavit is desirable, for it can be fyled in the Registrar's Office, and his successors can at any time verify the right of any person to the privilege of registration, without putting that person to any more trouble or expense.*

A certificate, under official seal and signature of any Notary Public, Mayor or Reeve in U. C., was formerly acceptable as evidence of qualification, but was found to be unsafe and impracticable; unsafe, because Reeves and Mayors could not discriminate between genuine and forged diplomas, and impracticable, in many cases, because the Act did not give the power to these functionaries to administer an oath in cases of doubtful identity. For this reason the law has been changed, so that the Registrar may require the affidavit to be made before a County Judge, if he is not satisfied without it.

The reason for requiring the production of the diplomas themselves, in preference to certificates, is that they may be marked in the Registrar's Office in such a way that either he or his successors could tell whether or not the same document had ever been registered before in the name of any other person.†

---

* The writer has, in many cases, registered persons whom he knew well without requiring the affidavit; but if his successor should not have the same personal knowledge, he would be perfectly justified in requiring proof. For this reason the writer has always required the affidavit from his own personal friends, and even those who graduated in the same class as he did himself, except where delay was likely to cause some loss to the person not registered. In these cases the formality has been occasionally dispensed with, the person being registered running the risk of being called upon by any future Registrar for the documentary evidence which is ordinarily required.

† In all these precautions there is an implied want of faith in the honor of applicants for registration. It appears like suspecting a person without sufficient reason. The writer has found several during his experience who have declined to register because of this implied doubt concerning them; and he has met with a good many others who have not forgiven him yet, even though as much care was taken to explain as circumstances would permit. Of course, nothing personal is ever intended in this generally implied doubt. Neither should the regulations be regarded as vexatious, for an officer, who like the Registrar, is liable to fine for falsification, cannot be too careful in scrutinizing qualifications. Independently of the danger of punishment, though, the Registrar is looked upon by the legitimate members of the profession as a sentinel placed at the gate of entrance to protect them from the intrusion of the unworthy. No one appreciating the

Section 31.

This section must never be lost sight of in construing section 41. It fully protects the registered practitioner from penalties for practising for "hire, gain," etc., but it does not protect him from punishment if he assumes a title which he is not lawfully entitled to.

The question is often asked, "Can a person who possesses the License of the Society of Apothecaries only, practise Physic, Surgery and Midwifery?—or, can a person who possesses the diploma of any one of the Royal Colleges of Surgeons of England, Edinburgh, or Ireland practise all three branches of Medical practice?" When the question is put in such a direct way, specifying a particular institution, it is within the sphere of a lawyer rather than a medical practioner to advise; but if a more general question is put, such as—can the registration of a diploma in Ontario confer any right or privilege upon its owner which it did not confer in the country in which it was conferred, there can be no difficulty in answering it? It does not. Registration does not create any new right, it simply legalizes the exercise of a right previously conferred.*

Section 32.

This section provides for the publication of a *Medical Register*. Under the repealed Act this was required to be done annually, but now it must be published as directed by the Council. It need not be at regular intervals.

Section 41.

This section is the one which the Registrar is most frequently called upon to explain. It is the one above all others which should be explicit and simple, in order that it might be understood by every Justice of the Peace. This it is far from being. This remark, the writer trusts, will not be considered derogatory to the gentlemen mentioned, when he adds that he has met with many lawyers who failed to grasp at once the full effect of this section. For this reason more pains will be taken to analyze and give a clear explanation of it than has been taken with any previous section.

A careful reading of the section reveals the fact that it creates three distinct offences, for which punishment is provided—*First*, a person may be guilty of wilfully and falsely pretending to be something which he is not—a Doctor of Medicine, for instance. *Second*, he may be guilty of practising for either hire, gain or hope of reward. *Third*, he may be guilty of falsely

---

responsibility of such a trust can regard it as more than the duty of the Registrar to exercise every power given to him, in order to test each qualification presented to him for registration. The convenience of an individual, though never to be disregarded, must ever be secondary to the interests of a community or corporation.

* The following is an extract from the preface of the Register of 1868. As the position then taken is legally sound, and has a general rather than a specific bearing, it is transferred to these pages in the form of a note:

"It can hardly be necessary to state that a diploma issued by any of the Medical Bodies of the United Kingdom, confers no right in this Province which it does not confer upon the holder while he resides in the United Kingdom. Thus, a diploma which qualifies its owner to practice either *Physic*, or *Surgery*, or *Midwifery*, does not entitle him to practice all of them when he registers it in this Province; but only the branch or branches which it entitled him to practice while he remained in the United Kingdom."

taking or using some name, title, addition or description which implies, or is calculated to lead people to infer, that he is registered according to law, or that he is a medical practitioner. For each of these offences he may be fined not less than twenty-five, nor more than one hundred dollars. Any one may be guilty of the first offence in some of its varied forms, but only those who are not registered can be guilty of the second or third offence.

The essence of the first offence is the wilful use of a title which does not legally belong to the person using it. The essence of the second is the acceptance or demand of a fee for medicine or services by any unregistered person. The essence of the third offence is the use of titles, appellations or descriptions which cause people to believe that the person using them is qualified to practise.

One thing which formerly operated greatly in favour of law breakers of all descriptions, was the right to appeal to a superior Court from the decision of a Magistrate. Convictions were commonly quashed in Quarter Sessions or County Court, because there was some technical error in the wording of an indictment or conviction. In consequence of this, "Quacks" in Ontario have had very nearly their own way. An impression prevails, to the effect, that it is useless to secure a conviction, even now, because of the danger of its being reversed in a higher Court. This danger, however, is not nearly so great as formerly—for a law was passed a year or two ago—which does not allow magisterial convictions to be quashed on account of purely techinical errors of the kind mentioned. If the facts are clearly of the nature of the offence with which a person is charged, and are proved by credible witnesses, the danger of quashing a conviction by appeal from the Magistrate is now—*nil.* While, however, this danger is so small it is not the less desirable that an indictment should be properly drawn up. The "offence" should be clearly stated, not in general terms, but particularly. Suppose for instance, that A. B. is charged with the first offence, above mentioned, it will not do to say that A. B. did wilfully and falsely pretend to hold a title which he does not hold, but, the particular title which it can be proved he did use must be mentioned. Suppose he called himself an M. D. without the right to do so, then the indictment should state "*that A. B. did wilfully and falsely pretend to be a Doctor of Medicine,*" inasmuch as he, the said A. B. did style himself as an M. D. in an advertisment, [or card, etc., etc., as the case may be,] *on the 1st day of June*, 1869, [or whatever date is correct.]

The essential part of the above is put in *italics.* The remainder relates to the particulars of the offence, which necessarily vary so much that it is impossible to more than indicate the style in which they should be worded.

The same remarks need not be repeated for the second offence, as there can be no misapprehension about it.

With regard to the third offence, it may be sub-divided into two—First, a person may lead people to believe that he is registered according to law. Second, a person may lead people to believe that he is a practitioner in medicine. People hear that a man is practising as a Physician or Surgeon they do not ask whether he is registered, or has complied with the law; they take for granted that a person who pretends to be a practitioner in Medicine is recognized by the law as such. The person who so misleads people is guilty of an offence. The indictment in such a case should state *that A. B. did falsely describe himself as a Physician*, Surgeon, or Practitioner in Medicine (as the case may be) *thereby leading people to infer that he is* recognized by law as a 'Physician,' 'Surgeon,' or 'Practioner in Medicine,' as the case may be.

Any person prosecuting should bear in mind the following points:

1. Never prosecute upon doubtful evidence.

2. Never prosecute for one offence when the facts are such as substantiate an offence of another nature.

3. Always see that the date of an offence is correctly stated, and where a number of dates can be given, always state that which can be sworn to by the greatest number of witnesses.

4. A person may be charged with all three of the offences created in section 41 of the Ontario Medical Act on the same day, and he may be fined to the full amount upon each indictment if the magistrate chooses.

5. Always employ a lawyer, unless the magistrate is particularly shrewd, or has had a large experience, even then it is best to employ a lawyer.

6. In employing a lawyer, select one with a good practice, for a lawyer may be learned in his profession and bungle a simple case through want of experience, either as to the mode of procedure or the wiles of a cunning adversary.

Section 43.

This section is the weakness of the penal clauses of the Act. The magistrate ought to have power to commit a person to gaol who does not pay his fine. However, the best must be made of a bad law until it can be improved. Some imagine, after reading this section, that only the Council can prosecute. This is an error. Any person may prosecute who pleases. If the person convicted does not pay the fine to the magistrate at the time, as he assuredly will not do if he acts under legal advice, he must be sued in either the Division or County Court for the amount of the fine. *This* suit can only be entered by an officer of the Council, and must be entered in the name of the College of Physicians and Surgeons of Ontario. No part of the fine is given to the prosecutor.

If a person who has been fined, "clears out" before the Court sits in which his case would be tried, nothing can be done. Let him stay away—the country is rid of a dangerous person, which is something gained. If, however, it is thought desirable to make him pay for the costs, it can be done if properly managed. We will suppose that A. B. has been fined $100, and there is reason to think he intends to leave the country for the purpose of evading the fine. The prosecutor, or somebody must make an affidavit setting forth the reasons which lead him believe that A. B. is about to leave the country. This affidavit must be taken as soon as possible to the Judge of the County Court, of the County in which the conviction is made, and if the Judge thinks the reasons stated a sufficient justification, he can order the arrest of A. B. and cause him to be incarcerated in the County gaol, until the fine is paid, or security given for its payment.

This affidavit should be drawn by an attorney, because any incorrectness in this might lead to an action for damages against the person making affidavit, on the grounds of a false arrest.

Clumsy as the Penal sections are, they are capable of efficient use.

Schedule A.

For a simplification of this Schedule see the table of qualifications which entitle to registration on page 49 & 50.